Long Lunch

a Montbretia Armstrong novella

Simon Cann

Coombe
Hill
Publishing

Published by Coombe Hill Publishing
33 Melrose Gardens
New Malden
Surrey KT3 3HQ
United Kingdom
coombehillpublishing.com

ISBN: 978-1-910398-10-4 (paperback)
ISBN: 978-1-910398-11-1 (ePub)

A big thank you to:

- Cathleen Small for her editorial input.

- Sarah Kruger (sarahkrugerdesigns.com) for the cover art.

19 March 2017

one

Near the old port.

Near.

Not at.

Not next to.

Not touching.

Near.

An unspecified distance away from.

You can't miss it.

Just plug the address into your phone and follow the directions.

Which would have been great advice if I had a smartphone, but I was the girl with a dumbphone and, like all dumbphones, my phone didn't do this map thing, so I had gone old school. I had used one of the computers at the hotel—in their pompously named business center, which in reality was a room with two old PCs, a fax machine that was switched on but covered with a layer of dust, and a laserjet printer that was about the size of a large suitcase. I had opened up the cranky old browser on one of the computers and checked the online map before printing it out.

The color map had rendered as somewhat unclear grayscale when the asthmatic printer spat out the page. I'd also printed out the page with Ryan's email message—his office address at the bottom.

For the record, "near" meant on the other side of the bypass or whatever they called it—the elevated roadway that threw into shadow the line between the old port and the city. The office street was, apparently, on the other side of the bypass, away from the old port, running parallel to the bypass. After five minutes walking up and down the street and concluding that the only color to be seen in Genoa was orange, I found the office.

Near to the old port. Near if you're a crow—or a seagull—and can fly. Near if you know where you're going. But less so if this morning was only your second morning in Genoa, and most of your time so far had been spent in, and looking at, the Cattedrale di San Lorenzo. The cathedral that was, with a certain irony, pretty darned close to where I had ended up.

"Hi, I'm here for Ryan Harris," I said to the receptionist. Carlotta Lombardi, according to the nameplate in front of her.

I guessed she was around the same age as me—maybe a bit more, maybe a bit less, but definitely twenty-something. And definitely of Italian extraction. She had the lightest dusting of olive in her complexion, and the tumbling curls and flowing curves were something painters had tried to capture for centuries.

The building was old, but inside seemed modern. The reception area had a high desk for Miss Lombardi, but everything else was low slung. The glass walls allowed a vision of a wide, open-plan office, but with the old building features retained, giving an idea of age but also breaking up the space to offer everyone his or her own area.

The goddess in training, or future artist's muse—I couldn't make up my mind which; all I could be certain of was that she wouldn't be answering phones and dealing with walk-ins from the street for long—replied. My Italian was limited. My accent was bad, so she immediately realized that my first language was American English. Her English wasn't perfect, but her English was much better than my Italian.

"He's not here," she said. The words were clear; the facial expression was confusing. I wasn't sure whether she was telling me apologetically or whether there was sadness. "He left at lunchtime."

"Oh," I said. "We were meant to be having lunch. When did he leave?"

"Monday," she said.

I couldn't help but smile at the answer. "No. I mean,

when did he leave for lunch?"

"Monday," she said, her curls bouncing as she repeated her answer, confident that she had understood me and was giving the correct answer to the question I had asked. "He left at lunchtime on Monday."

"But today's Wednesday," I said. "When did he leave today?"

"He didn't," she said. "He left on Monday and hasn't come back." She waved her hands from side to side, trying to emphasize the non-return, then softened her face to smile as she tried to sympathize with my embarrassment: "A long lunch."

"I'm sorry. He left on Monday—at lunchtime—and you haven't seen him since?"

"Sì," she said. "I mean yes: He did not come back. Am I saying it right...in English?"

I felt my face relax, telling me I was getting angry at her when it wasn't her fault. "Your English is perfect," I said. "It's Ryan who's confusing me. He said to meet him here...today."

"Here?" asked Carlotta Lombardi.

I felt to the back pocket of my jeans and pulled out the printout of the email, unfolding it and putting it in front of her on the desk. "This is what he sent me. Yesterday."

The goddess leaned forward to read the email, giving me a view of the top of her head and her perfectly sculpted cleavage. Her head moved from right to left, following each line of my email exchange with Ryan. Like a typewriter, at the end of each line her head moved to the start of the next, her curls shimmering under the artificial light as her head moved.

"That's the correct address," she said, laying a finger along the bottom of the printout. "When did he send this?"

"Yesterday."

"Are you sure?" she asked. Then, realizing she was contradicting me, she panicked slightly. "I'm sorry. I don't know the right words in English...what I mean is...I know it arrived yesterday, but did he send it before? Did it get lost...

delayed...in the internet?" She shrugged—whether at her perceived lack of English vocabulary or her lack of capability to explain technology issues, I wasn't sure.

"I only arrived on Sunday evening," I said. "I was going somewhere else but decided to come here for a few days. I posted a message on Facebook on Monday morning—this email came on Tuesday, because of that Facebook message. So even if it got lost..."

The receptionist finished the sentence for me: "He still meant yesterday or today—both after Monday." Her hesitancy fell away, and she switched to efficient receptionist mode. "Let me see if anyone else has seen him."

She rang two people. I'm not sure whom, not that it would have made any difference to me. She then talked—quickly and animatedly—in Italian. When she hung up, she looked dejected. "No one has seen him since Monday lunchtime."

That was it. She was out of ideas. She was back to her role as trainee goddess tending the phones and greeting visitors.

"You read the email," I said. "He mentioned a fish restaurant. Any ideas which one he might be thinking of?"

She said something quickly and in Italian. I pulled out the map printout and laid it in front of her. She reared back—like me she found varying shades of gray hard to differentiate between. "Could you mark it for me, please?"

She spent a moment or two focusing on the scrap of paper. Without taking her eyes off the page, her right hand went out, feeling across the desk, returning when she had found a pen. "We are here," she said, putting a red circle. "The trattoria is here." She put another red circle.

"Could you write its name?" I asked. "I'll just spell it wrong."

She looked up at me and smiled. "The sign fell down last year. It's opposite an American bar—find the bar and you'll find the trattoria. At the main door..." She pointed as if explaining how to get out of the office, "Turn right—here...I've marked the route. It will take you three or four minutes."

two

It took more than three or four minutes.

The incorrect estimation of time was not a matter of fault by the goddess-like receptionist, who for a goddess had been very approachable. Instead, it was a matter of trying to read the map that I had printed using the hotel's clunky old printer.

In the short time I had been in Genoa, one thing I had found is that there are few flat areas. The city is a long, thin strip: on one side, there is the sea, and from the sea the land rises sharply to form a mountainous region, which eventually meets up with the Alps. The old port is, unsurprisingly, next to the old part of the city—that being the medieval quarter rather than the Golden Age quarter. I was learning that the medieval quarter—not that anyone apart from me seemed to call it the medieval quarter—was characterized by narrow lanes. *Carrugi*, someone at the hotel had told me they were called. One carrugio, several carrugi, apparently. I was learning that the carrugi and physical geography of the city worked together to form something like a real-life M C Escher picture: No matter which way you walked, you always seem to be going up.

"Take the funicular," they said. Now I understood why.

I followed a carrugio—one of the minute filaments on the map, indistinguishable from its neighbors on the now-battered piece of paper. Having ascended what felt like a near-vertical narrow lane between the tall buildings for five minutes, passing under several bridges linking the two sides of the narrow lanes, I was unwilling to cede any of the height advantage I had gained, which meant I made a few more bad decisions.

After ten minutes, I found myself in the Piazza De

Ferrari, a grand square built around a central fountain and surrounded by magnificent, imposing buildings: probably once palaces, but now bank headquarters. There would be time to do the tourist thing and to appreciate some level ground, but first, there was a trattoria—without a sign—to be found.

I retraced my steps, found my mistake—a turn too soon—and was soon standing with my back to an American bar, feeling warmer and slightly stickier than I had hoped to feel. It was the end of March, but the climate in Genoa—much as it had been when I left Barcelona—was pleasant. If anything, Genoa felt warmer: It was the perfect temperature for strolling around and looking at the sights. Less perfect for a fast walk.

Carlotta Lombardi was right. There was no sign outside the trattoria, but on the stone lintel above the door that I guessed was the main entrance, there was an oblong shape with curved corners that was less weathered. To the left of the entrance was something that might have once been a menu holder, but that too seemed to be out of service.

There were three tables outside. Also old, and with the sunlight cut off by the tall buildings to either side of the carrugio, I could see little to encourage their use today. However, in the middle of the Mediterranean summer, the cool offered by this quiet backwater would be appealing. Assuming the American bar didn't get too loud.

At first I thought my entrance had silenced the place—like in an old Western when a gunslinger walks into a bar in an unfriendly town. As I stood in the gloom, it took a few moments for me to realize that the natural state of this place was quiet. At each table, there was one person—individuals eating lunch. This wasn't a place people came to be social; this was a place that people came to eat, to enjoy food. The sound of cutlery tapping on porcelain was the only regular sound.

A waiter passed, carrying a plate too small for the cooked fish it supported. He delivered the plate to a table at the far side of the small room and returned, passing me without comment. He passed again: another plate, a different variety of fish, delivered to a table closer to where I stood.

Again he returned, passing me as if I was invisible.

"Excuse me," I said, using English without thinking.

The waiter turned. His look was neither friendly nor unfriendly, but there was no hint that he was trying to welcome me to the restaurant. His English was poor but functional. "Not for tourists," he said. "Menu in Italian."

He might as well have said, "Go away, we don't want your sort here." I understand the message. I tried to smile my most disarming smile and responded in my stuttering Italian: "I'm looking for my friend—we're going to eat lunch here...he says it's very good. The best fish in Genoa."

I wasn't sure what amused the waiter the most: my awful grasp of Italian, my dreadful Italian accent, or a line that sounded like complete bull. He scanned the room and looked back at me. "No Americans here."

I searched my limited Italian vocabulary, trying to figure what to ask him next.

"Come in. Come in," he said, waving me into the room. "Look. No Americans... Do you see your friend?"

I scanned the room. Older men, one woman, all dining alone at small tables, apart from one couple.

I reverted to English. "He's not here."

He gave a nod that said, "I know; I told you that, but you wouldn't listen."

"Thank you," I mumbled, "I'm sorry to have taken..."

He waved a hand, the international language to say no problem.

I returned to the narrow alleyway to ponder my next move.

three

On days like today, I regretted not having a smartphone so that I could have my email and messages with me all the time. But using dumbphones while I traveled kept my costs down: I didn't pay for the phones—my collection had been acquired from friends upgrading to smartphones—and if a phone got lost or damaged, then I just took another recycled phone from my bag. Plus, I didn't have to worry about paying for data—I could use a simple pay-as-you-go type arrangement, the biggest expense being sending text messages to my sister Ellen, who was in London.

I didn't want to schlep around internet cafés, so I returned to the hotel and borrowed one of the computers in the business center to examine the email again. Even though I had printed it, I wanted to make sure there was nothing else that I had missed, and I wanted to check whether there had been a follow-up email or if something had fallen into my spam folder.

Definitely today. Definitely Wednesday. Definitely meet at his office.

The goddess of the reception desk was arranging some brochures as I arrived. She had the kind of figure that I had always wanted—that I think most girls want. The kind of figure that I had always expected, or at least hoped, to grow into. Curves everywhere. Enough, but never too much—the ratio between each dimension perfect.

Instead, I had grown up skinny. Not that skinny is bad. Skinny—or athletic, as they say when they're trying to be complimentary—has a lot of advantages. But there's always that slight twinge, that feeling of being second best or not quite measuring up when you meet a goddess. And if not second best, then at a disadvantage.

She looked sad to see me again. Whether this was

frustration or empathy, I wasn't sure. Maybe all goddesses were perpetually disappointed when they encountered us mere mortals. Especially when we wore jeans, sneakers, and white cotton blouses, and not the figure accentuating dress that she wore. Maybe she found my straight, brown, shoulder-length hair too uninteresting when she felt her lush curls bounce as she moved her head.

"I went to the trattoria that you suggested," I said. "No luck."

She mouthed "oh," but I didn't hear any sound.

"Would anyone else... Could I speak to...?"

Her face dropped but somehow became more official. "Oh, I'm sorry, the conference rooms are all booked this afternoon." It was a line she was clearly used to using. An excuse that could not be argued against.

Goddesses: one; mortals: nil.

"The people you spoke to... The people who know Ryan... Could I speak to them?" I asked. "I don't need a conference room—I don't need confidentiality."

Goddesses: one; mortals: one.

She was calculating. Argue or give in. If she argued, would I give in? This was the second time I had been there, and I hadn't respected her previous excuse, which could not be argued against. She gave in and picked up a phone.

Goddesses: one; mortals: two.

She said something in Italian and hung up. "She'll be out in a moment."

"Thank you," I said, trying not to grin at my tiny victory over the goddesses.

The glass door leading from the reception into the open-plan office area opened. A woman, maybe thirty, stood. If you took the goddess's proportions and added two inches in every dimension, but dropped a few inches in height, and then topped that with a round face and dark frizzy hair, this was what you got.

"This is Elisabetta," said the receptionist. "She's Ryan's boss." She turned to the boss, who was stumbling to respond.

"This is…"

"Montbretia," I said. "Call me Monty." Someone once told me that there was a British general in the Second World War called Monty. Apparently he had been part of the invasion of Italy. I wondered whether the same thought was going through her head.

"Mon…" she said.

"Mon—bree—shuh," I said slowly, figuring it better to use my full name. "It's a flower."

"Elisabetta," she said, smiling and holding out her hand to shake. "You're a friend of Ryan." She looked over my shoulder to thank the receptionist. "I'm not sure what I can tell you, but come through."

She led me between some desks into what seemed like a gloomy corner of the office without any natural daylight. Immediately the area looked different—in the main span, there were small aluminum laptops on most desks; here, enclosed within white plaster-faced walls on three sides were three desks arranged in a U-shape, each with a huge monitor.

"This is where Ryan works," she said, pointing to the desk on the left. "Sit down, please." She indicated his chair and sat at the chair at the next desk, turning to face inward.

I sat, turning the chair inward.

"And this is Tommaso," she said, pointing to the back of the third chair. The chair spun to reveal a young man with a weak beard and a weaker smile. "Welcome to the art department." She turned to the weak beard. "Mon-bree-shuh is a friend of Ryan."

The weak beard nodded as if it was an everyday occurrence that the guy who sat behind him would disappear and forty-eight hours later a complete stranger would turn up asking questions, but he didn't say anything. And neither did Elisabetta. Both sat, staring at me, waiting for me to speak.

"I'll give you the short version," I said. "I arrived in Genoa on Sunday evening, and on Monday morning I posted a note on Facebook saying I was here. On Tuesday morning…

yesterday...I received an email from Ryan telling me he was working in Genoa and inviting me for lunch. Today. When I got here, Carlotta at reception told me Ryan left at lunch-time on Monday and hasn't been seen since."

Both nodded. They looked between each other, as if confirming their understanding, and nodded again. Neither spoke.

"I was wondering if you knew where he was," I said.

The weak beard shook his head without needing to consider the question.

"Or if you had any idea about why he isn't here," I tried.

Elisabetta exhaled. "I'm not sure what we can tell you."

"You're his boss," I said. "What's he like to work with?"

"Boss," she snorted. "There are three of us: I've been here the longest."

The weak beard nodded, as if claiming status as an equal.

"He gets in late, does his time, goes home early," she said.

"It's like he's got a wife who keeps him on a short leash," said Tommaso in a short snarl. His English was surprisingly good with hardly any accent. Elisabetta frowned, looking at Tommaso, who slumped back into his seat, regaining his silence.

"He does good work," she said calmly. "He's very creative. He always impresses everyone." She waved a hand loosely, as if indicating the people outside the three walls. "He does his hours...and then he goes home."

The gloom deepened. Where the fourth wall would be—where the natural daylight came from—a man was standing. Tommaso immediately spun back to his desk, as if it wouldn't be noticed that he hadn't been working. Elisabetta stood and stepped toward the man, who was in buff chinos with a blue open-necked shirt.

The conversation was intense and in Italian. I turned my chair to face Ryan's desk. As I spun I knocked a small pile of papers that had been stacked at one end. It had the look of what one might find in a pigeonhole—I guessed the three members of the art department would retrieve the contents of each other's pigeonholes.

There were some memos, all in Italian. The red cross on one made me guess at a first aid or safety notice. I didn't pay much attention; what grabbed me was the crisp white window envelope. In my experience, window envelopes in offices only have one use—pay slips. And here was an envelope with a sheet of paper inside, printed and addressed specifically to Ryan with a street address that wasn't the office.

I tidied up the pile as Elisabetta returned, looking slightly flushed from her conversation. She muttered something under her breath. I wasn't sure what she said, but I guessed it wasn't complimentary about the man who had just departed.

While she muttered, I folded the envelope in half. "I've taken up enough of your time," I said and stood, slipping the envelope into my back pocket.

four

I bought a street map—it seemed the better option, given the state of the piece of paper in my pocket and its propensity to lead me astray.

The guy selling maps and tat that only tourists would ever buy didn't understand my need to open up each different map. "This is Genoa," he said. "Do you want the big map or the small map?" I didn't really care how big the map was—I wanted the map that included Ryan's street. The fourth map he had—medium size but much smaller scale, requiring excellent eyesight—was the right choice.

I paid, oriented the map against the streets, and threw myself back into the carrugi. After about fifteen minutes, I had passed out of the carrugi and into a more modern part of town. The streets were wider—wide enough to fit a car, but not wide enough that you'd want to drive fast or meet a car coming the other way—and the buildings—mostly blocks of apartments, almost all covered in orange-hued render and probably dating from the fifties or sixties—were set back from the road. There were fewer stores but no tourist attractions, which is what I wanted and expected from a residential area.

The address on the pay slip was an apartment block: four floors high, a flat roof, and rendered in a darker orange hue. The ground-level entrance led to a stairwell that opened up onto open passages that ran across the front of the building.

There was no bell and nothing to draw attention, so I rapped with a fist.

No response.

Four PM, not surprising. People should be at work.

I rapped again.

There was the sound of movement—feet coming toward the door. The door swung open slowly. I knew men had a problem when they encountered a beautiful woman—or at least a woman they believed to be beautiful, which usually meant a woman they wanted to sleep with, which for the average male meant about ninety-nine percent of the female population—but feeling this way was a first for me.

The boy that answered—and while he was probably in his twenties, you could only describe him as a boy—was the most beautiful male I had ever seen. His face was soft and round, with his lips permanently puckered in an "oh" shape as if he had just received a mild surprise. His hair hadn't seen a comb that day, but the blond locks had a casual just-got-out-of-bed look that most female models spent hours perfecting.

I stared. I couldn't begin to think why I was there. I was captured by the beauty of this boy and unable to think or communicate, or even breathe. I was snared, and he wasn't even trying. He had opened the door and stared at me—there had been nothing to imply that he was pleased to see me or that he was interested in who I was; he simply stared.

Eventually he said, "Ciao."

I tried to shake myself and failed. I found my mouth worked, but the rest of me, especially my eyes, was transfixed by this beautiful, beautiful boy.

"I'm looking for Ryan," my mouth said without my brain giving it instruction.

"He's not here," said the beautiful boy.

I started to take control of my body: I could move my head, but my eyes had still declared independence, refusing to be torn away from the beautiful boy. "Are you his..." Something in my brain was screaming to be discreet. I knew Ryan's sexual preferences, but it wasn't my role to out him. "Are you his...roommate?" I asked.

The beautiful boy snorted and indicated the white toweling robe he was wearing, encouraging my eyes to notice that he was barefooted. "I'm not his cleaner," he said. His English was heavily accented, and I suspected he had never bothered to improve his diction. He was too beautiful to have to worry—everyone else would bend to his will.

"When did you last see him?" I was taking control of my whole body now, but my eyes still wouldn't look at anything but the beautiful boy who shrugged.

"Aren't you worried?"

He twisted his lip.

"When does he usually get home?"

The beautiful boy sighed. "He gets up before I'm awake; he comes home late. What can I say? I'm not his mother."

It took me a few seconds to realize that the beautiful boy had shut the door on me, and I was standing alone on the open passageway.

five

I stopped in the first café I reached and had a coffee. The coffee was good, the coffee refreshed me, but it didn't help me figure out where Ryan was or why he'd set up a lunchtime meeting at his office when he hadn't been there for two days.

After the coffee, I made my way lazily through the carrugi to the hotel. I could try another email to Ryan or see if he was posting anything on Facebook that would give me a hint as to what was going on.

The glass doors slid open, and I stepped into the lobby. I took three steps: "Surprise!" The female voice was familiar, but the context was wrong, and I was still thinking about that beautiful, beautiful boy. "Monty!" The female voice was more insistent. I turned. I recognized the figure—a woman with a suitcase—but she wasn't meant to be here: Ellen was meant to be in London, not Genoa. Ellen didn't do impulsive, spur-of-the-moment things, and yet here she was.

I threw my arms around her. "What are you doing here, sis?"

"You said, 'Come and see me in Genoa.'"

We both stepped back to look at each other. "I said, 'Sister, come and see me in Barcelona.' I said, 'Sister, come and see me in Brazil, Patagonia, most of Southeast Asia and Australia and New Zealand.'"

"I..." she began.

"Don't explain. Just give me another hug; it's been too long." When we released, I continued. "Have you got a room?"

"They were just..."

I stopped her. "My room's got two beds—share with me, and then you can tell me everything that's going on."

"You're sure? It won't...?" She was hesitant.

I ignored the comment and headed for the desk. It took

less than a minute to arrange a second key card, and then I picked up her case. "Welcome," I said as I led Ellen into the room, hefting her heavy case onto the second bed. "You get in the bath—I'll unpack."

It didn't take long to understand why Ellen's suitcase was so heavy.

Most tourists arrive with a guidebook: a slim volume filled with flowery prose, offering a view of the city that is probably ten years out of date. Ellen, a history professor, had arrived with several of what looked like encyclopedias for individual buildings. Maybe a whole five hundred pages dedicated to a single church, offering a view that was five hundred years out of date.

I let myself into the bathroom and put the lid down on the toilet before sitting. Ellen was in the bath, bubbles up to her neck. "So how are you?" she said, in the way that only older siblings can pull off. She didn't need to use words; her tone alone expressed genuine heartfelt concern, but with slight disapproval at implied and unspecified reckless behavior.

"You mean Barcelona," I said. Ellen had waited until I was if not trapped, at least obliged to sit in one place. She used to wait for car journeys to have these conversations— two people stuck in a tin can, neither able to get out, and because of the need to keep eyes on the road, you can just talk without looking at each other. And she wasn't looking at me here—she was focusing on washing and relaxing—but Barcelona was a conversation we were going to have, whether I wanted to or not. However, there were probably details that I could leave out because it would just take too long to explain and she wouldn't want to hear the explanation anyway—like about the guy I left tied to my bed on the night I departed.

"I want to hear about Barcelona," she said. *That* tone had slipped from her voice. "Everything. I'm sure you enjoyed yourself there... But that can wait—I'm here because I wanted to see you. It's been too long, and I thought it would be fun to see Genoa together."

"The medium-sized municipal library in your case told me that you're interested in Genoa."

Ellen smiled. "So what have you been up to since you arrived?"

"It's been an odd day," I began. "I was supposed to meet a friend for lunch. A guy I knew while I was in college. He's a couple of years younger than me—he was a fine arts major who moved to become a designer."

Ellen splashed in the bath and listened.

"He said to meet him at his office. Today. At 1 PM. When I arrived, he wasn't there."

"Oh," said Ellen. "That's a bit rude."

"It's more than that," I said. "The people in the office last saw him on Monday, as in the day before yesterday Monday. But he sent the invitation to meet him for lunch yesterday."

"I'm intrigued. I also have that sense of dread," she said. "There's a scab you've been picking at. A wrong that has to be righted." There was a slight tension in her voice again.

"I just asked the people he worked with, that's all." Ellen seemed to relax, and I continued. "They seemed to think he had a wife at home who kept him on a tight leash."

"And?" said Ellen. Experience had taught her that there was always likely more.

"There's no and," I said. "There's no wife. Ryan is gay."

Ellen went as if to ask a question but held herself back.

"And before you ask, no, he's not a little bit gay; no, he's not in denial about something else; no, he's not bisexual or whatever. He's just gay."

"Being gay doesn't stop him having a partner who keeps him on a tight leash. A tight leash isn't something that is exclusively issued to women on their wedding day."

I sighed. "Yeah, I know. But the assumption that he had a wife distracted me. It made me..." Ellen didn't react, so I continued. "I went round to his apartment."

"You're..." Ellen began. That tone again. She stopped.

"I went to an apartment—the apartment of a friend—in

the middle of the afternoon, in a crime-free area, and knocked on the door. It's not even on the scale of risky behavior," I said, predicting my sister's thought process.

The movement of water around Ellen's shoulders told me she had shrugged.

"The boy who answered the door," I felt myself floating as I recalled the beautiful boy, the golden locks around his cherubic round face. "I say boy...I mean man—he's probably my age—but he is beautiful, he was..."

Ellen coughed intentionally. "This afternoon. Not fantasy." Her tone was mock stern. "But if you want me to get my own room, you just need to..."

I was still thinking about the beautiful boy. "His view of Ryan was different to what they said at the office. He said that Ryan gets home late—the office people think he leaves early, and I'm left wondering what happens in between."

"But this doesn't explain why he set a lunch date and then didn't show," said Ellen.

I pushed out my bottom lip and shook my head.

"Well, you can be assured that your dinner date tonight won't stand you up. But she could do with a towel."

six

"This," said Ellen. "This." She was pointing with her finger, as if tapping a bar in front of her. "This behavior. This need to find something wrong in the world and then to try to fix it—even if it doesn't need fixing. *This* is what worries me."

And to be frank, *this* wasn't the first time we had had *this* conversation. *This* wasn't the first time we had had *this* conversation in Genoa.

"I just want to spend some time with my sister," she said. She held back, knowing that the guilt-saturated follow-up question—"Is that so bad?"—would just provoke the situation.

"You are spending time with me," I said, as bouncily as I could. "Come on, Ellen! You're on vacation—do something different. Don't be a historian for once. Or if you have to be a historian, be a grateful historian."

"Grateful?" asked Ellen, unsure of the line I was following.

"Grateful that I'm showing you a part of town that isn't in the history books. Think about it, you're going back to the source. How often do you get that?"

Ellen mumbled something. She knew better than to try to argue. If she had wanted a different outcome, then she should have stated her case before we left. Not that she realized where we were going or what my intention was. But my lack of specificity in explaining where we were going should have been enough to set off a warning siren for her.

"Okay," she said slowly. "I'm grateful. But where are we? And don't say Genoa."

I pulled the map I had acquired this afternoon from my back pocket, unfolded it, and pointed with my nose. "Here."

"And what is here?" she asked, weighing each word, cautious not to agree to anything further.

"This," I said as we reached the orange-hued apartment

block. "Ryan's apartment." Ellen shot me a look of disappointment. "I just want to check," I said, leading her up the stairs. "He might be back."

Ellen acquiesced. I knew she wanted to ask what I was going to do if he wasn't home, but I also knew that she knew that was a pointless question—she would find out if he wasn't there, and there was always the chance that he had returned.

I rapped on the door. Ellen stood three paces away, looking awkward and embarrassed. I rapped again, giving Ellen an apologetic smile. I could hear steps from within. The door opened, and the beautiful boy was looking at me.

He was different. He had washed his hair—it was still damp with the golden locks slicked back—and he had shaved. The harsh blade that had been near his perfect skin was only given away by the nick on his jawline.

He sighed heavily and said nothing, letting his eyes question. I should have introduced Ellen—the two would have been in agreement.

"Has he...?" I began.

"No."

"The third night, and you're not..."

He cut me off. "As long as he pays the rent." He shrugged.

"Do you have his number?" I asked, holding up my phone, which I had hung on a lanyard around my neck.

He shrugged. I waited, still holding up my phone. He shrugged again and turned into the apartment. I followed him and let the door close behind me, leaving Ellen outside.

seven

I didn't set a stopwatch on it, but I'm certain I was inside for less than two minutes, and probably more like 90 seconds.

"That," said Ellen. "That." She was pointing at the now-closed front door of Ryan's apartment, and yet somehow the finger seemed to keep swinging toward me. Each time it was too close to being pointed directly at me, Ellen would consciously swing her pointing finger toward the front door. "That behavior. That sort of risk. That worries me."

I threw my arms around her and kissed her cheek. "And that is why I love you, sister. Now...you were taking me to dinner." I released my embrace and turned for the stairs.

Ellen followed three steps behind, finding it hard to keep up and simultaneously berate me. "You took these stupid, crazy risks in Barcelona—and look what happened there."

"Look what happened in Barcelona?" I asked. "Ultimately nothing."

"But...you..." said Ellen.

I didn't want to have an argument with my sister in the street, but her *tell me in your own time when you're ready* attitude seemed to be wearing thin. I slowed my pace so that she could keep up and we could continue moving. We might end up arguing in the street, but at least we wouldn't be having a shouting match at one fixed point, somewhere outside an orange-hued apartment block.

"Sure," I said. "There was a lot of potential for trouble in Barcelona. But nothing happened." It was a lie, but I had to stay consistent with the lie I had told her before. The lie I had told her when I was shocked and scared. The lie I had told her when I had left a man—a man who I was sure wanted to have sex with me, there and then, irrespective of whether I consented—tied to my bed.

I had told Ellen it had been a bad neighborhood with

dubious characters. Unspecific language, unspecific danger—I let her imagination create the situation.

I could have tried to explain to Ellen why I didn't simply run and instead chose to tie up the guy, but I wasn't sure that would make her worry less. I might even convince her, but that didn't mean she wouldn't worry. And it didn't mean I had done the right thing or the smart thing.

Confronted by a man who had drunk too much and was angry enough to want to rape me, I had made a choice. I could have run. If he had caught me, my running would have provoked him, and I'm fairly sure how that would have ended up. If I had gotten away, then I would've had to leave everything behind. My money, my passport, my clothes. Everything.

So I took the other option: I let him think he was in with a chance. I told him I would give him a night to remember. And I was true to my word. I tied him to my bed, packed my bags, and left Barcelona. When I got into France—France, because I was so scared that I ran to another country—I asked the friend who had driven me to arrange the rescue of the guy I had tied to my bedframe.

Was that sensible or was that the riskiest thing I could have done?

I still wasn't sure. And without being sure, or at least having a better idea of whether I thought I had taken the sensible option, I wasn't going to discuss all the options with Ellen.

"I had to go into Ryan's apartment," I said.

Ellen was torn between admonishing me and wanting to hear my explanation as to why I *had* to go into the apartment.

"I may have accidentally picked up Ryan's pay slip while I was at his office this afternoon." I smirked. "I needed to put it somewhere safe."

"Monty," said Ellen, the tone disapproving. No, scrub that. The tone way beyond disapproving.

"But you saw the boy, the beautiful, beautiful boy...."

"Actually, I didn't," mumbled Ellen discontentedly.

"Well, you should have," I said dreamily. "You would've seen that he couldn't hurt anyone. Plus I learned a lot."

Ellen was still mumbling.

"First, I learned Ryan's phone number." I held up my phone that was hanging from the lanyard around my neck, showing Ellen Ryan's contact details. I punched the call button. "Hi Ryan, it's Monty," I said when his voicemail picked up. "It's Wednesday evening—give me a call when you get this message."

"It hasn't really moved you forward," said Ellen dismissively.

"Knowing Ryan's number may not illuminate the puzzle Ryan has created for me. However, knowing that the beautiful, beautiful boy is called Gianmarco made my heart skip a beat."

Ellen sighed. "You've been calling that name silently in your head since you found out, haven't you?"

I flushed.

"What did you do?" asked Ellen. "Say 'Hi, I'm Monty, what's your name?'"

The flush turned to a crimson blush. "No. There was a stack of mail—I put the pay slip in with that. The letters that weren't addressed to Ryan were addressed to Gianmarco Rossi."

"Rossi?" said Ellen. "And so you were testing Montbretia Rossi?"

The crimson blush started to burn. "I was...and then I counted the beds in the apartment. There's only one bed: Gianmarco isn't Ryan's roommate—he's his boyfriend."

Ellen sighed and shut her eyes. "And you're... No, stop." She looked at me, fixing me in her glare. "I know where your mind's going—but please stop. Can we just go and have dinner? The two of us, together. No talk of Ryan or the beautiful Gianmarco."

eight

"Can I be a dull and tedious historian for one moment?" said Ellen as our coffee cups were cleared away. She rummaged in her bag and put a few bills on the plate the waiter had left. "No one *just disappears*. No one disappears, or should I say, no one is made to disappear without leaving something in their wake."

"I know I haven't found anything, but that doesn't mean he isn't in trouble."

Ellen was doing her *I'm going to be patient because you're not bright enough to understand* thing. "Look to Ryan. It's far more likely that he decided to go away for a few days."

"No. You're wrong, Ellen. "Something has happened." I could hear my voice getting more strained. Ellen didn't reply—she no more wanted an argument than I did. "You haven't told me what's happening with Nigel," I said, changing the subject to one of her friends back in London.

"Nigel is being very Nigel," said Ellen. "Everything— *everything*—is about that book of his. The publisher has appointed a PR guy to look after him. 'Boniface, my PR guru,' says Nigel, getting himself all puffed up."

"Getting himself puffed up and not realizing that you've already published a book that has sold quite well and is into its third print run. Not to mention, you've had PR people running around for you," I said.

"Some things are best not mentioned to Nigel," she said. "He's a sweet guy, but there's a reason why he's going to spend the rest of his life alone."

"There are several reasons," I said as the waiter picked up the small stack of cash Ellen had placed.

"More than several reasons," said Ellen. "But let's not..."

"That was lovely, thank you," I said, indicating the now empty dinner table.

"You're sure you don't want anything more."

"I want more," I said. "The question is whether I would be physically capable of eating more. And the simple answer is no, I wouldn't."

The temperature felt much cooler than it had when we entered the restaurant. I pulled my jacket tight, knowing that Ellen wouldn't want a fast walk back to the hotel, so I wouldn't warm myself that way.

After we left Ryan and Gianmarco's apartment, we had made our way back toward the heart of the city, along the way taking a few wrong turns when our attention was focused on our argument more than the direction we were heading. We had found ourselves on a wide street. Ellen had checked the location on her phone and said something about the history of the road.

Whatever she had said had passed me by—I was still thinking about Ryan.

There was a colonnade on each side of the road, providing a covered walkway. To one side of the walkway, stone arches, and on the other there were shops—mostly aimed at tourists—and restaurants. Ellen had suggested one of the restaurants along this stretch, and it had been a great choice.

Ellen was looking at the colonnades, comparing one side of the street to the other. "Look," she pointed. "On one side, a single choice of stone, but with detailed ornamentation—see the intricate carvings." She looked for traffic, then stepped into the road, pointing up at the arch. "On the other side, a far simpler design with little ornamentation, but..."

"Stripes," I said.

"Stripes," agreed Ellen. "Layers of black and white stone." She scrunched her face, giving that disappointed look. "It would have been nice if they had the same architectural design on both sides."

"Look." Something—or rather, someone—had caught my eye. I tugged at Ellen's sleeve, releasing it quickly since it made me feel like a five-year-old.

On the other side of the road—the black-and-white

stripes side of the road—there was a man walking. There were several men, but one stood out. "Golden hair," I said.

"In this light, blond maybe," said Ellen. "You mean curls and the light-colored jacket."

"Trust me," I said. "The hair is golden. And yes, the light jacket. Come on."

I grabbed Ellen's sleeve again and tugged.

"Are you going to explain?"

"That's Gianmarco," I said as the beautiful boy disappeared from view behind a black-and-white striped pillar.

"Monty," hissed Ellen. I started walking, then picked up my pace until I was diagonally across from Gianmarco. There was the sound of unwilling footsteps behind me— Ellen feeling obliged to keep up. "What are we doing?"

"Following," I said as Gianmarco left the colonnade and turned right. I grabbed Ellen's sleeve and checked the road for traffic. "Come on, we're crossing."

"Monty, this is..." We turned the corner. The main street hadn't been busy; the side road was quieter with an occasional car and only one other pedestrian—Gianmarco who seemed to be out for a leisurely walk, except that I knew he was some distance from home, and he seemed to be walking with intent.

"You're not going to tell me this is dangerous," I said to Ellen, keeping my voice so the beautiful boy, about thirty yards ahead, wouldn't hear. "I'm with you, so we must be safe."

"Being near you isn't a guarantee of safety," said Ellen, slipping her arm into mine.

"Then think of this as an opportunity to view history in the making," I said.

Ellen harrumphed but didn't slow her pace. "If we're going to follow him," she began, "shouldn't we be on the other side of the road? You know, to make it look more... casual?"

I couldn't hide my grin of pride as we crossed the street, keeping Gianmarco in our sight.

Ellen was trying to form a question. "How... Wh... Who... Why are we following him?" she finally blurted.

"If your boyfriend was missing, would you be out? Dressed like that?"

"Dressed like what?" asked Ellen. "And how do you know he's not looking for Ryan?"

Gianmarco took a left turn and dropped out of sight. "Quick," I said, dragging Ellen to a light jog. We reached the street where Gianmarco had turned—it was narrower than our street, virtually a carrugio-width, without sidewalks, but wide enough for a single vehicle to pass.

Gianmarco headed up the street, his pace seemingly slowing. Then he turned and disappeared inside a building. "Now can we go back to the hotel?" asked Ellen.

"Sure," I said. "Once..."

Ellen sighed and pulled me back as I went to move. She tilted her head to the left. It took a moment or two to see what she was indicating: a second man, more heavily set, dressed darker than Gianmarco, was following the path Gianmarco had followed. He turned into the narrow street, and when he reached the point where Gianmarco had turned, he too disappeared.

"Come on," I said and started following down the narrow street. The acoustics changed with the tall buildings being so close together, and as we approached the disappearing point, the sound of music—a pounding beat without melody—became louder, but not necessarily clearer. At the place where the two men had disappeared was a dull, glowing yellow light.

Ellen pushed us to the side of the street farther from the yellow light. In practice, this meant she walked down the center of the narrow street, rather than me. Each step closer, we slowed, virtually stopping as we drew level. It was a doorway that opened onto a sharply descending stairway. Inside the door, a man wearing a tuxedo stood, looking bored. Outside the door, the only ornamentation was a vertical sign on the left of the doorframe: Spartacus.

"Behind," said Ellen, pushing us forward. Having moved about twenty or thirty yards past the entrance, Ellen reduced the tension on my arm, allowing us to stop and spin round. Two further men disappeared into the yellow glow.

"What do you think?" I asked.

"You're the expert," she said, "but I don't think our womanly charms will help us here."

I couldn't argue with her.

"Can we go back to the hotel now, Monty? You can send Ryan an email from there, or perhaps try calling him again."

nine

Ellen looked peaceful as she slept.

She was sleeping deeply: I got up, used the bathroom, and dressed, and the noise I created didn't disturb her. Then, in an attempt to make sure she stayed asleep, I turned off the alarm on her phone and left her.

I took the map, but it stayed in my back pocket—I knew the direction I was heading, and most of the route was familiar. In the bright morning light, I could distinguish that each of the orange-hued buildings was a slightly different shade of terracotta, apricot, peach, and cream, but it still took a while until I recognized that I was following the course I had followed twice yesterday.

The apartment block was still when I reached it. Still, but not silent, and there were lights on in several of the apartments. In other words yes, it might be early—and I was hoping it would be early for Gianmarco—but it wasn't outrageously early.

I rapped on the door.

Silence. The lights remained switched off.

I rapped again, more heavily and for longer.

No change.

With the next rap, my knuckles told me they'd had enough, so, seeing no signs of activity within, I took to pounding with the heel of my hand.

A light. A change in the light as if a body had moved in front of it. Then footsteps. Flesh moving slowly.

The door cracked. A bleary eye looked through the crack. "Let me in." I pushed the door. Gianmarco jumped back as the wood knocked into his skull. He muttered something in Italian as I closed the door behind me.

He was still indescribably beautiful, but for the first time, I saw a hint of what he could become. The baby soft skin on his rounded face—still showing the creases from where he had been lying—seemed to sag in the morning. It was almost, but not quite, puffy. He was on that knife edge where youthful vigor passes to *normal*. Some guys start as spotty little kids and acquire some sort of gravitas as they age. I had a vision of Gianmarco being the opposite—he was beautiful now, but in ten years, he would just be fat.

"He's not here," he said, seemingly becoming uncomfortable with the investigation my eyes were carrying out. "All night, no sign."

"And how was your night?" I asked, standing in the small hallway, hoping to be offered a coffee.

He muttered something in Italian. I think it translated to, "Okay, I suppose."

"You didn't go out?" I asked, looking at the bedroom door, which was ajar. Yesterday, when I pushed my way in, it was open—that had allowed me to see that there was only one bed in the apartment.

He said something in Italian. My limited grasp of the language was already exceeded.

"Tell me about Spartacus," I said.

"It's a movie," he said quietly, pulling his robe tighter. I let my gaze fall on him and waited. "It's a club." He sounded like a surly teenager.

"So I ask again, how was your night last night, Gianmarco?" When he didn't respond, I continued. "I saw you going into the club."

"You followed me?" For the first time that morning there was some animation in his voice.

"No," I said. "I didn't follow you. I went for dinner with my sister. As we left the restaurant, you walked in front of us."

The indignation faded, but he didn't say anything.

"Is that how someone reacts?" I asked. Gianmarco frowned but didn't say anything. "Your boyfriend goes missing, so you go out to a club. Your boyfriend goes missing and you get dressed up and go out to a hook-up place."

"He's not my boyfriend," said Gianmarco. I raised my eyebrows but said nothing. "He's not."

"I've known Ryan long enough," I said. "You don't need to hide it from me."

"He's not my boyfriend," insisted Gianmarco. He deflated. "He was... He was my boyfriend, but not anymore."

I wanted to sit down. I wanted Gianmarco to sit down and tell me what had happened. I looked into the kitchen, hoping to see somewhere we could perch and some way to get a coffee. There were plates on every surface. Plates with old bits of food, congealing and drying. No pots or pans had been used—just plates, each with a knife that was equally dirty.

I quickly counted the plates: fifteen.

I turned back to Gianmarco. "When did you break up?"

It seemed too much effort to shrug. "Two weeks ago, maybe."

His eyes were moistening. "What am I going to do now?" he asked. "Who's going to pay the rent?"

"What happened?" I asked softly, ignoring his concerns. This time he shrugged.

"But he moved country," I said. That was a fact; where I was less clear was whether Ryan had moved country to be with Gianmarco. Such a move would be consistent with Ryan's impulsive behavior and his not always realistic romantic dreams. "Did he move to be with you?"

Gianmarco nodded, still visibly upset. I couldn't make out whether he was upset by the breakup, by Ryan's disappearance, by the fact that he'd been caught clubbing, or because the rent wasn't going to be paid. I suspected the latter, but maybe there was something deeper. Maybe Gianmarco was beginning to understand that he was no longer the freshest peach and now he was alone. Perhaps the secret behind the bedroom door was that there was no secret.

"Tell me what happened," I said.

ten

The sun had aligned with the path. For just a few minutes, the sun was filling the narrow gap between the tall buildings on each side—its rays directly hitting the small open area outside the office.

I sat—cat-like—in the bright sun, soaking in the warmth. It was March in Genoa: The air temperature in the morning was warm enough, but the mercury was not recording what you would call Mediterranean temperatures. For walking around, it was a pleasant warmth—not too cold and not so hot that you broke into a sweat just getting out of the hotel lobby. But in the narrow alleys with the high buildings, it felt damp, and that damp feeling made it seem as if the temperature fell by another ten degrees, so I was pleased to sit—purring—in the sun as I waited.

A lot of people passed, all heading into the office. As far as I could tell, Ryan's firm, a small marketing agency, only had one floor of the old building. If I was right, then many of the people passing wouldn't know Ryan. They might recognize him by sight, but they probably wouldn't have the firsthand experience I was hoping for.

There was a mop of unruly brown hair. In the daylight I could see the line where natural color met bottle color. Elisabetta saw me, took a moment to recognize who I was, and came to join me in the sun.

"Mon-bree-shuh. Have I got it right?" I smiled broadly. "Any news?" she asked.

"Something and nothing," I said. "I've seen his... roommate who..."

Elisabetta looked mildly surprised but didn't seem to have any appetite to fill in the gaps of my hesitation.

"Something his roommate said didn't quite chime with what you and Tommaso told me."

"Oh," she said, her eyes becoming wide.

"You said he left on time every evening."

Elisabetta nodded earnestly.

"His roommate says Ryan doesn't get home until late."

"Oh," said Elisabetta again, her eyes opening yet wider. "So where does he go?"

"That was my question for you," I said.

"Oh," said Elisabetta. I willed her to release the muscles that seemed to be pulling her eyes wider open.

"Did he drink? Did he go out with you? Who were his friends? There must be something you can tell me," I said.

"Hmmm," said Elisabetta tilting her head and bringing up a hand to support her chin. I looked at the somewhat overweight woman and wondered: Was this the future for Gianmarco? Give him five or ten years, would he just be a dumpy lump?

"Do people like him? Do people respect him? Is he good at his job?"

Elisabetta brightened. "He's very good at his job—he's very..." She stumbled as she sought the correct English words. "Talented. Creative. He has the best ideas."

This sounded like the Ryan I knew. In college, all the bands asked him to design their posters, their logos, their T-shirts, and anything else they could think of, because they knew Ryan had the best ideas.

"But did people like him? Were they friendly with him?"

A slightly snide smile crossed Elisabetta's face. "Not Tommaso." I waited. "Tommaso had been with us for eighteen months when Ryan came. Tommaso is very..." She frowned, questioning whether she was using the term correctly: "Workmanlike? Is that the phrase? Am I saying it right in English?"

"You mean he can use the computer programs but he doesn't have the artistic flare?" I offered.

"Exactly," said Elisabetta. "And so when Ryan came, it made Tommaso look..." She struggled. "How would you say? Ryan became number one; Tommaso moved down to number two."

"So Tommaso wasn't a friend, but it sounds like others had noticed Ryan. Were they friendly or did they just respect Ryan for the work he did?"

Something rippled across Elisabetta's face. Not quite discomfort. Not caution. But something had unconsciously tripped a warning. "He seems very friendly with Lorenzo Mariani." As she said the name Lorenzo Mariani, there was distaste.

"Who's that?" I asked.

"Mariani? He's a client. Well...I think he's a client. We do work for him, but I'm never sure how much income he generates for the firm. He's one of Vittorio de Santis' clients." Her tone became more matter-of-fact. "Vittorio's one of the senior guys—you saw him yesterday."

"Blue shirt, chinos? Made Tommaso go stiff?" I said.

A single nod of her head.

"And does Vittorio like Ryan? Is he friendly with him?"

She exhaled, considering. "He certainly respects him—he won't let Tommaso work on any of his accounts. I'm not sure whether he's friendly. They're very...different."

"So if he's different from Vittorio de Santis, what about Lorenzo Mariani?"

There was that look of distaste again.

"Are they friendly?"

"They got on..." said Elisabetta haltingly.

"But?"

"Mariani isn't the sort of...he's not like our other clients." I waited for her to offer more. "His business is different." She seemed done on the explanation.

"Different?" I asked. "Do you mean a different...industry? Or do you mean he's part of the mafia?"

"No, no, no, not that," she said, quickly checking behind her. "Although... No." She composed herself. "I don't think he's...criminal, but..."

"And Ryan was friendly with him? Ryan knew him? Ryan got on with him?" I pushed her.

She considered her response. "Ryan dropped off his

work in person. Most clients we email—but Ryan printed out the label or whatever he had designed, and he took it to Mariani."

"Is that bad?" I asked.

"Not bad. Just...different."

"Where do I find this guy?"

There was shock on her face. "You don't want to...it's not a nice..."

I pulled the map from my back pocket. "Show me."

eleven

"I want to spend time with my sister."

I wondered whether Ellen had calculated: Try emotional blackmail, appeal to reason if that fails, and if she still didn't succeed, then come along unwillingly.

"And I want to spend time with you," I said, "but I also want to find out what's happened to Ryan. If anything's happened to him, then I don't think I could...knowing that with five minutes of my time I could've helped."

Two of us could play at that emotional blackmail thing.

Ellen had suggested we go out for breakfast. We found a small café in the old port and arranged ourselves so we sat side by side, allowing us to both look out at the world as it went past. "Don't you think you're getting a bit obsessive," she said. Grammatically, her words were structured as a question. Her tone of voice, however, offered no question mark at the end of the sentence. "You get up and before breakfast go and wake up Ryan's boyfriend..."

"Ex."

"Ex," she said, exasperated. "And then you interrogate his work colleagues."

"I didn't interrogate. The office was on my way back—I just sat in the sun and waited." I took a sip of my coffee and continued to stare across the harbor.

"Why don't you call the police?" asked Ellen.

"Because," I said. Ellen didn't say anything, but I could feel her lean forward, expecting some explanation. "Because they won't care. He's an adult. He's not an Italian national. I can't even prove that he's missing. And my Italian isn't good enough to answer all the questions they would be bound to ask."

"So let me get this right," said Ellen, talking slowly, taking on her *I'm going to lay out the basic facts for you, you stupid person* voice. "Ryan and Gianmarco have broken up. Ryan is not in the home shared with Gianmarco. Ryan missed a lunch with you, which is enough for you to devote every waking hour to finding him...but that's not enough to call in the police, or the carabinieri, or whatever we call in here. Do you see my point? It's either important or it's not—if it's important, we call the police; if it's not important, then why are you wasting your time?"

"I'm not wasting my time." I could hear the sharpness in my voice.

"Bad choice of words," said Ellen, trying to soothe. "If it's not important, then why can't you spend the time with me?"

We both fell quiet, looking out over the harbor as if we had chosen to be quiet. Around us people in the café chatted, and there was the gentle clink of porcelain on porcelain, punctuated by cutlery on porcelain.

Eventually, Ellen asked, "Didn't you have enough of this in Barcelona? And those bags in the room—they aren't yours."

"One morning," I said. "I just want to spend one morning looking for my friend. Come with me, and this afternoon we'll do the whole historian-on-vacation-showing-her-feckless-sister-the-sights thing."

I turned to look at Ellen. Uncertainty screamed from her face. "Come on," I said. "It'll be good for you. You'll get to see how Italians think and act—it will inform your understanding of history."

twelve

"Are you sure you've got the map the right way up?" said Ellen. "We could follow the directions on my phone. Wasn't it you who told me I needed to get a phone that did all the clever things? Wasn't it you who set up my phone to do all the clever things?"

"But technology likes to make up its own mind," I said. "Elisabetta told me to take this route. She says it's easier to see the entrance."

Ellen had agreed to spend the morning with me—or at least, what remained of the time before lunch with me—looking for Ryan. In reality, that meant we could knock on one door: Lorenzo Mariani's. "Are you being sensible?" Ellen had asked.

"Of course I am," I said. "I'm going with you. I could have just gone on my own, but instead I persuaded you to come. Give me some credit."

Some credit… In truth, after I had spoken with Elisabetta, I was hungry, and the thought of breakfast reminded me that I had left Ellen asleep. Rather than have the argument, I went back to wake her so that we could have breakfast together.

Ellen was awake and having a shower when I got back to the hotel, so I could argue perfect timing on my part. Instead, we went to breakfast and argued about whether I was doing the sensible thing.

After breakfast we had dived into more narrow alleyways, starting near the old port again, but moving away from Ryan and Elisabetta's office. Initially, the alleyways were broader—still narrow, but broader. Wide enough to fit a car. Wide enough for the booksellers to have their stands permanently on the side of the track—huge metal boxes with lids that opened to create a serviceable market stall. And between the boxes and the far wall, there was still enough room to get a car through. Not that any car would want to pass through the milling tourists.

As we moved farther up the hill, the tourists dissipated and the alleys narrowed.

"Show me where you think we are," said Ellen, pointing with her head toward the half-folded map in my hand. "And should you really be waving that map around like that? Doesn't it scream *tourist*? Didn't you say that we should be careful, and...?"

I stopped walking.

"Do you see any thieves?" I asked.

"Doesn't mean..."

I sighed, cutting her off. "Hold that side of the map," I said. Ellen took the far side of the map, giving me a free hand to point. "We started here."

"Yes," said Ellen.

"Walked up here. The bookstands were here. And we turned left here."

Ellen was nodding.

"So we continue up. Second right, and it should be straight in front of us. Agreed?"

"Agreed," said Ellen.

I took the map and folded it before returning it to my back pocket. "There. We no longer look like tourists. And by the way, it's not street thieves that concerned Elisabetta—it's the prostitutes."

"Oh." Ellen's mouth made a perfect circle, mirroring Elisabetta's reaction to my questioning earlier.

We carried on walking, taking the second path on the right. Ellen's pace slowed—this was her way of asking a question but without asking a question. They say most communication is nonverbal; we transmit context and emphasis through our body language. If someone ever needed a case study, my sister Ellen was perfect.

"What?" I said.

"It should be..."

"Just ahead," I said. "And yes, I thought it would be more obvious." There were a few very rundown shops. Each shop was shallow—more like a stall built into the wall with roll-down shutters. In front of us, fruit and vegetables had been arranged, but there seemed to be no shopkeeper.

"Shall we go back?" asked Ellen.

"No," I said. "They'll know." There were two women, probably into their forties: stilettos, lacy stockings, short skirts, and plunging necklines assisted by push-up bras to reveal ample amounts of cleavage.

It was the cleavage that gave away their age. When I looked closely at Gianmarco's face this morning, I noticed how his skin was starting to lose its freshness. Some of the firmness was starting to weaken. When he talked, his skin moved, and as it was pulled taut, the signs of strain under the surface were beginning to show.

And so it was with these two women. It was more than the sun damage: their cleavages—their shop windows, just like the grocer's fruit and vegetable—put on display their over-ripeness. This was fruit that was spoiling; this was fruit for making jam. It wasn't the sort of fruit that you would want to eat, unless you had a sharp knife or you were cheap.

"*Scusami*," I said with my limited Italian. "Do you speak English?" I had a feeling that their English would be limited but that they would know a lot of English words that I had no conception of.

Neither responded. They looked at us as if assessing fruit on the fruit stall.

"Lorenzo Mariani," I said.

They looked to each other, then laughed.

"Not you, honey," said the taller of the two, stepping toward me, her dangling earrings catching up as she turned her head. My jacket was unbuttoned—she took a lapel in each hand and opened the jacket as if theatrically drawing back stage curtains, then stared down at my blouse. "No," she said with a thick Italian accent.

She took half a step back, looked to her friend, then

turned back to me, her earrings still in motion. "He likes…" She held her hands in front of her chest. "Bigger." She looked over at Ellen, focusing on her chest. "Undo" she said, miming as if to undo two or three blouse buttons. "And smile, honey."

She stepped back and started to turn away.

"Where do we find Lorenzo Mariani?"

"Who?" she asked. Her friend who seemed to be wearing even heavier lipstick smirked.

I reached into my pocket and pulled out the first bill I found: €20. They were like heat-seeking missiles. Their focus was immediate and total.

"Lorenzo," I said, holding the bill at eye level. She reached for the bill; I pulled my hand back. "Where?"

She pointed back toward the fruit and vegetable shop. I frowned. She pointed and moved the pointing hand to the left. She repeated several times.

"The door on the left," I said. She nodded, then held her hand flat and pushed it forward, moving it up an invisible slope. "Upstairs?"

She nodded and grabbed the bill. "He likes bigger." She shrugged and walked away, arm-in-arm with her friend, laughing.

thirteen

There was no sign to suggest that my €20 had been well spent, but through the peeling dark-green frame, the door was open.

The staircase was narrow, dimly lit, and uncarpeted. I led. Ellen expressed her disquiet nonverbally.

The stairs opened onto a small space that just about qualified to be described as a room. Like the rising wooden treads, it was uncarpeted. There were two windows, but it looked like a long time since they had been cleaned, and now they just functioned as two dull squares where some daylight pushed its way through.

There was a desk. Old. Wooden. Solid. With some character. In front of the desk there were two old wooden chairs, and behind the desk sat a man. He was about thirty; olive skin, which was well weathered; and dark curly hair.

"Lorenzo? Lorenzo Mariani?" I asked.

There was a sound behind me. Ellen finally catching up.

The man behind the desk sat quietly—his eyes were doing the work, scanning both of us. He lifted his left hand, holding it up and forward like an orator about to say: "I believe." He stared at me and turned his hand, encouraging me to turn sideways.

I turned.

There was a tightening around his mouth. A disappointment.

"Are you Lorenzo?" I asked again. He lowered his hand and said nothing. "I hear you're a friend of Ryan Harris."

There was a moment of confusion. Whatever he had expected me to say, I hadn't. Whatever he had expected hear, he hadn't expected to hear Ryan's name.

"I'm in Genoa for a few days and I was hoping to catch up with him."

He sat still. Behind me, Ellen shifted uneasily, her feet scraping on the bare wood boards.

"I was hoping you might know where Ryan is," I said.

When he spoke, Lorenzo's voice was soft. "I don't really know him. I've met him once or twice, but..."

I tried to look at the papers on his desk. Papers. No computer. It made some sense that Ryan would come here; sit on the chairs in front of the desk, which looked uncomfortable; and show this man his work. But it wasn't clear how a man who, according to two prostitutes, had a preference for larger-busted women was then doing business that could take advantage of Ryan's skills.

"I heard you know Vittorio de Santis, too."

It wasn't a snort, more an exhalation of air through his nostrils. "I know..." He paused and sat back in his chair. "You seem to know a lot."

I waited.

"If you know so much, why don't you know where Ryan is?"

I continued waiting. Ellen shifted her feet, I could hear her unvoiced plea to just get out of the small lightless room.

"I'm not sure I can help you," he said.

"If he happens to stop by, could you get him to call me?" I asked.

"Certainly." It was a positive response, but his tone was negative.

"Don't you want my number?" I asked. "So that he can call."

"If he knows you, then he'll know it." The conversation seemed finished.

fourteen

I would see something and say, "Wow, that's pretty." Ellen would see something, and there would be a whole historical background. An influence seen here that had also been seen there. A new technique that spread because a clan moved due to persecution. An invasion and subjugation of a people and the imposition of new gods.

To me, everything looked old, apart from the stuff that had been added in the last 70 years—and most of that just look horrid.

To Ellen, there was no new and old—there were simply layers and events on a continuum from the beginning of time until now. But she was the historian, and I was the girl traveling around the world.

I knew there were two parts of Genoa, but I struggled to differentiate. Ellen explained but did little more than repeat what the guidebooks had already told me. Il Centro Storico, the old part of the city, fanned out from the old port. This made sense to me.

But then there was Le Strade Nuove, the new streets. In this context, new meant sixteenth century: the buildings built when the city state of Genoa was at the height of its powers. I had no difficulty with this as a notion. My difficulty was calling five-hundred-year-old architecture *new*. Surely at some point in the last five hundred years, the new streets were accepted as *the streets* and the prefix *new* went to be applied to some more recent architecture.

And it wasn't just the naming that got me. Intellectually, I had no problem with the concepts. Emotionally, the two areas didn't feel different to me. On the ground, they didn't look a whole heap different.

"So now we're in Le Strade Nuove—the new streets," said Ellen, looking at me across the table. We had found a restaurant that looked like somewhere we could get a light lunch. I felt it was only polite to let Ellen choose the quarter and the venue: I had rather dominated the morning's activities. This was near to a church or cathedral...some religious place that Ellen the historian wanted to see. "It smells different, doesn't it?"

"What? This restaurant?"

"No." Ellen laughed. "When you move from Il Centro Storico to Le Strade Nuove, the smell changes. It's...it's... fresher, cleaner.... You can smell the sea here..."

It was Ellen's afternoon. I wasn't going to pick a fight about the smell of Genoa. I'll argue my case if I care about something, but honestly, I hadn't noticed any change of smell, and even if Ellen was right, I didn't know which side of that argument I was on.

The waiter came. "Order for me," I said. Ellen was struggling to decide what to have—she couldn't choose between two dishes. This way, she didn't have to choose—she could order both and have half of each. Me? I just wanted food.

"You're looking glum," said Ellen as the waiter disappeared. "Don't be. You did all you could. You asked that guy above the fruit stall..."

"Lorenzo Mariani," I said.

"You asked Mariani about Ryan, and he told you a lie. But you've got to let Ryan be an adult and make his own mistakes."

"But Ryan's not an adult," I said. I immediately wanted to take it back—it wasn't that it was wrong or an unfair mischaracterization of my friend: It simply didn't reflect the point I was trying to make.

"And while you infantilize him—while you run after him, treating him like a child whose problems need to be fixed and can only be fixed by a responsible adult—you keep him as a child. Let him grow up. Force him to grow up and sort out his own problems."

Ellen was right, but she was missing the point. Not that she was to blame for missing the point; I had sent her in the wrong direction. However, her admonition was starting to get old—I had given way and was following her, so it was time for her to stop pecking away at me.

She went to say something more. I stopped her. "He lied. To me."

"Ryan?"

"Probably, but, no..." I said. "Lorenzo Mariani lied to me. To my face."

Ellen seemed exasperated. "Now who should grow up? An unpleasant man in an unpleasant office in a seedy part of town with prostitutes outside tells a lie. It's not going to make the front page of the newspaper. It doesn't even make an interesting chirrup...or whatever those things are with hashtags."

My sister the historian. She can cross the road and notice a shift in architecture or a slight change in the smell, but present her with modern technology and ask her to explain its current significance, and she stumbles.

"You're missing my point, El. He lied to my face," I said. Ellen made a big show of shrugging. "My point is not that he lied."

"So..."

I cut off Ellen. "He lied. I get that. I accept that. I have no problem with him lying."

"You could've fooled me," said Ellen.

"But why did he lie for Ryan?" Ellen looked confused, so I elaborated. "If he told a lie for himself, I'd understand. But he admitted to knowing Ryan, so why lie about how well he knows Ryan?"

"Perhaps because..." began Ellen.

"I'm going back," I said. "I'm going to ask him."

I stood. Ellen spluttered something.

"I'll catch you up," I said.

fifteen

There were no prostitutes outside the office, at least none that I saw. No one to tell me that they thought my breasts were inadequate.

The dark staircase was no more appealing than it had been an hour before, but now I knew what I was walking into.

There was a flick of recognition from Mariani, who was still behind his desk in the gloomy room. "It's you," he grunted. I didn't reply—I just sat on the farther of the two uncomfortable-looking chairs in front of his desk. The chair was every bit an uncomfortable as I had expected it to be. "The other one could've made more money."

I felt my face flinch—he saw the confusion and explained. "The customers like to grab..." He made a pawing motion with his hands. "You might be prettier than the other one and younger...but you need tits." He leaned forward, his voice dropped as if offering sage advice. "I know a guy whose girls are into the really dirty stuff—I can put you in touch."

I wasn't sure if he was telling the truth or just trying to disorient me.

"You know my friend, Ryan Harris. You know Vittorio de Santis, who works with Ryan."

"But I don't know you," responded Mariani without waiting.

I laughed at him and made sure he understood I was laughing at him. He sat in his chair, his gaze fixed on me—it was the only source of warmth in that room, not that he seemed concerned about the temperature.

"Seriously," I said. "You're worried about me. A girl like me? You're going to tell your friends that you're scared of a girl?"

I'm never a fan of demeaning myself, but I find when

I'm dealing with a man who may not be as evolved as the sisterhood would hope, it's often best to lessen myself, at least in his eyes. Nothing changes for me—I'm still the same person—but if calling myself a girl instead of a woman is sufficient to let him drop his guard, if only to prove his manliness, then I'll go for what I'm after.

There was a pause; then he started to thaw, a hint of a smile crossed his face.

"I'm a friend of Ryan," I said. "I'm here for a few days and want to see him." Mariani nodded, as if to demonstrate he could be empathetic. "Is Ryan in trouble?"

There was a twitch. An involuntary spasm.

I turned my head slightly, letting him know I had seen something. Letting an implied question be asked.

"No," he said with little conviction.

"No, Ryan isn't in trouble, or no, you didn't just react when I saw you react after I asked whether Ryan's in trouble?" He seemed to be struggling with my question, which was the intention. "Or yes, he is in trouble, but no, you're not going to tell me about it."

He was even more confused. His English was good, but not good enough when I was trying to mess with him.

"Why don't you just tell me what sort of trouble Ryan has found?"

Mariani began slowly, picking his way through a minefield of opportunities for me to willfully misinterpret what he was saying. "He's not *in trouble*."

"But there is something," I said. "You know something."

"Cards," he said.

"Gambling?" I asked.

Mariani nodded. "I think there's a girl." I waited for him to elaborate. "He said he wants to get married...said he'll get married overseas...and he was talking about adopting a kid, so I thought he was trying to pay for...I don't know the English word, but when they stick it in the woman."

"Fertility treatment," I offered.

He smiled. "Yes, that! I thought he wanted money for

fertility treatment. Am I right? Is that why he wanted the money?"

"I don't know," I said. "Until I've talked with him, I won't know."

Mariani looked slightly dejected.

"So does Ryan have gambling debts?"

He snorted dismissively. "Thousand. Two thousand, perhaps."

"Two thousand euros," I said, with more alarm than I intended.

My reaction seemed to amuse the man on the other side of the table...but I was just a girl, so I wouldn't understand these things. "That's not much. He's owed more...he's won more. It's not enough to disappear and have a girl..." He stopped, his lower jaw twitching. "You...you're...you...you're not...not his girlfriend...?"

I tried to smile with him, not let him know that I was laughing at him, again. "I'm not...and I haven't been undergoing fertility treatment," I said.

He relaxed visibly.

"So, assuming he's not run away because whatever he owes isn't that much, then where is Ryan?"

Even in the gloom of the room, it was easy to see the self-satisfied grin as it crept across Mariani's face. "If I knew that, I'd tell you to stop you coming back."

sixteen

I was already in the shit with Ellen—she was bound to shout at me when I next saw her, so I figured I might as well put off that moment.

Mariani was wrong.

Mariani was wrong in fact—there was no girlfriend, and I was pretty sure that there was no fertility treatment—but I suspected he was right in principle.

And while I couldn't really get into much more trouble with Ellen—her anger generally reached a plateau—I wanted to know whether Mariani was indeed right in principle. One man could tell me.

I rapped on the door.

There was the sound of movement, and the noise of the television was muted. When Gianmarco opened the door, he was dressed as he had been when I first saw him yesterday, which is to say he wasn't really dressed. He was wrapped in a white toweling robe, and I suspected he had been sitting, hypnotized by daytime television.

"I was worried about you," I said. "Can I come in?"

He stepped back from the door, neither inviting me nor trying to stop my progress. He looked different from how he had this morning. Maybe it was me—in fact, it was almost certainly me, no one ages that swiftly—but he looked changed. He was still beautiful, but that beauty had changed.

He was beautiful compared to the average, not beautiful as an absolute. He was better than most, no longer the perfection by which others are judged. It was like the scientific conundrum—does observing something change it? When Gianmarco was not being worshipped, did his beauty start to ebb away slowly, then more quickly? Was his weakness inattention—was he the flower that wilted without the sun, or did he just fear that once he was ignored, then no one would ever notice him again, and did that eat him up from the inside?

My eyes followed the path they had followed this morning, being drawn to the kitchen.

He noticed that I had noticed.

"Can I wash your dishes?" I asked.

There was confusion on his face. He didn't understand the question, he couldn't see my motivation, and he clearly didn't grasp the value of the task.

"Please," I said. "My way of saying sorry for barging in here."

His tone was noncommittal. "Do what you want."

I led. He followed, probably because he wasn't sure what else to do. "Trash bags?"

His face was blank. I was a stranger from a strange land talking about things he had never heard of.

I started opening doors under the counter that ran along two walls. At the end of the row I found the cabinet that exists in every kitchen: the place where the cleaning materials are stored. Front and center there was a roll of trash bags. I tore one off and opened the sack as if I was testing a parachute.

Clearly this was a custom that was only known to the people in my far-off and strange land.

"Hold that," I said to Gianmarco, indicating how I wanted him to hold the black polythene. He reluctantly stood in the doorway and took the bag, holding it as I began scraping the detritus from the dried plates. When the sink was emptied, I began to fill it—this time with water, adding a squirt of dish soap.

"Tell me about you and Ryan," I said. "It may help me find him...it may help to get your rent paid."

Giving him the trash bag had brought him into the kitchen, but now, mentioning his rent, I had his attention. He still didn't seem ready to talk.

"Where did you meet?" I asked.

"Sharm el Sheikh." He was holding the trash bag, but now he was waiting. He knew this simple answer to a simple question would grab my attention.

"But..." I began. He could see that I was trying to process the information and form a question but was struggling. "That's not the most gay-friendly place I can think of."

"Precisely," he said, smiling broadly.

"Not that you're restricted to gay-friendly places or can't..." I quickly added, stopping when I felt I was about to start over-apologizing or expressing how unfazed I was with the lifestyle. I moved on quickly. "Why there?"

"The guy I was with wanted to get some sun. He thought it would be a good idea. I think Ryan's guy had a similar idea. We were in the same hotel—both with boring boyfriends—and we found a way to pass the time."

"When was this?" I didn't want to know how they had passed the time.

"November."

"November? As in November, last year?" I counted in my head. "Four...five months ago."

"Five," he said.

The sink was full, so I turned off the faucet and put the plates into the hot water to give them a few moments to soak while I continued my investigation into the countertop.

"When did Ryan move here?" I continued.

"December." I felt my head involuntarily spin. I was no longer looking at the countertop; I was now staring at Gianmarco, wordlessly questioning him in quite an aggressive way. "December," he repeated. "Six weeks after we met—to the day—Ryan moved to Italy."

"That was fast," I said. "Clearly the attraction was strong."

And clearly, Ryan had lost none of the impulsiveness that I had seen in him when we had been at college. Gianmarco seemed to be blooming as he told the story. As he recounted the story of a man pursuing him, some of his beauty returned.

"And this apartment?"

"Ryan visited twice before he moved over," said

Gianmarco. "We found it on the second visit, but it wasn't ready until January because of Christmas and New Year. But that was good because he didn't start the job until January."

"Do you work?" I asked. I was pretty sure of the answer, but I felt I needed to check—Ellen would be disappointed with me if I didn't.

Gianmarco shook his head. A tiny movement that would be more appropriate for an Edwardian English lady in a BBC period drama who was refusing sugar in her tea.

I looked away. I wanted Gianmarco to feel a level of privacy before I asked the next question. "Everything started quickly. Everything was good?"

He made some sort of sound as if to affirm.

"Then how did you go from good to fallen apart?"

"Let's buy a place—we need our own home. Let's get married—but we have to go abroad. Let's start a family—we can adopt. Now. Now. Now. But he was never here—he was always working." The explanation came as a flood.

seventeen

Carlotta Lombardi did not disappoint me.

Maybe she had received the sunlight of attention and so hadn't wilted.

She recognized me as I walked in and smiled broadly, remaining seated behind her desk, which was raised so that the goddess could survey the rest of her dominion—the reception area of the office where Ryan worked. "Ciao," said the goddess, perfect in every way. "You're Ryan's friend."

"Montbretia," I said. "But I'd like to see Elisabetta."

Something drew my eye as she reached for the phone to her right. I was powerless against the allure of the goddess, and maybe it was this allure that drew the constant adoration that nourished her. Or maybe she was truly beautiful—on the outside at least. I had yet to discover whether she was more than physically striking. But for the moment, she certainly had the kind of figure with the right curves that Lorenzo Mariani would approve of.

She hung up. "Elisabetta will be right out."

I felt sorry for Elisabetta. I liked her—she had been friendly, she had been helpful, she had been concerned about Ryan. She was intelligent and seemed to have an understated but quite biting sense of humor. She had her own style, but when you put her next to Carlotta Lombardi, all you could see was a shapeless lump.

"Thanks, Carlotta," I said as Elisabetta arrived. I hustled my host away before she could be directly compared to the goddess. "I want to keep you up to date on Ryan."

"Okay," said Elisabetta leading me across the edge of the open-plan office toward the three white plaster-faced walls where the art department was confined.

"Hi, Tommaso," I said to the second member of the art department. He spun in his chair—still the weak beard and again the weaker smile.

He mumbled something.

"How are you today? Are you working on anything interesting?"

His face brightened, and I'm sure that the beard made something resembling a smile as Elisabetta and I took our seats.

"I thought it might be useful to tell you what I've found about Ryan," I began. Tommaso's face soured, and he turned back to his work.

"Mmm," said Elisabetta.

There was a change in the light—a figure was standing where the fourth wall would be, acting like a fourth wall. I heard the sound—like the sound someone makes when they want to shoo a cat—before I looked up.

When I looked, I saw Vittorio de Santis. He was wearing buff chinos with a blue open-necked shirt. Similar to yesterday, but probably slightly different.

Elisabetta was standing, and without speaking she pushed past me. I went to follow Elisabetta but felt a hand on my shoulder. Not heavy, not invasive, more an emotional instruction than a physical restraint.

"Have you finished my work yet?" said de Santis to Tommaso.

From observing the back of his head, I could tell that Tommaso was flinching. He raised a hand to point at his screen. De Santis leaned to look, releasing the hand from my shoulder,

"That's shit," he said. "Leave us." He jerked his thumb to indicate movement to anywhere that wasn't here. "You not working will give us better results."

The weak beard couldn't hide the red face as Tommaso slinked away. The senior man dropped into the vacated seat.

De Santis had the look of a man who enjoyed his food, but who might still do some exercise. Not enough exercise to reach the point of equilibrium where he burned off all the food he consumed, but enough exercise to ensure that he retained some physical stature.

However, to his credit, he did not seem to be using his physical bulk to intimidate me. He let his anger do that work. When he spoke, his heavily accented English could not mask his contempt. "Why are you disturbing my client?"

I didn't understand the question. That probably showed on my face.

"Don't play stupid," said de Santis. "You're the American girl who has been looking for Ryan."

Now I understood his question, I felt my face flush at my embarrassment for not having understood what, in retrospect, was a very straightforward question. "You mean your client Lorenzo Mariani?"

Vittorio de Santis forced an exaggerated smile.

"I didn't realize he was a client," I half lied. "What business is he in? Why does he need your help?"

"He's moving into the fruit export business—he needs packaging," said de Santis, cutting himself short.

"Can he afford your fees?" I asked. "This office must cost something to run..."

De Santis winced.

"Mariani's business seemed...modest."

Vittorio de Santis straightened in the weak-bearded graphic designer's chair. "I'm sure you will understand that the nature of our business relationship is covered by confidentiality agreements."

It seemed strange that he wanted to bring up confidentiality now, but I understood the basic message he was trying to convey: This topic is closed.

He leaned forward—not enough to be obnoxious or aggressive, but sufficient to make sure he had my attention. "Our clients don't matter to you. Our business is of no interest to you. You're meant to be Ryan's friend, right?"

I felt frozen, unable to answer.

He waited.

"I am his friend," I said, eventually, not quite sure what else to say.

"Then don't keep coming here. If you're his friend, it must be obvious what's wrong in his life, so help him."

eighteen

"I am so, so, so sorry. When they write the history books, there will be one volume dedicated to the worst sisters in history. There, on page one, at the very top of the list, it will say: Montbretia Sylvia Armstrong. She neglected her sister Ellen in the historical city of Genoa; she is without doubt the worst sister in history."

Ellen's face remained motionless.

"Shit, just my luck having a sister who's a historian. You're already writing that book, aren't you?"

There was a slight flicker.

"Please tell me that you at least enjoyed looking at... whatever it was you've been looking at."

A slight softening.

"I had to go and see Gianmarco..."

Ellen closed her eyes as if they would hold back the torrent of anger. It didn't work. "So you went to see that unpleasant man..."

"Lorenzo Mariani," I said. "And by the way, he's still got work for you, if you want. Men like to grab..."

"You go and see this Mariani and then you go and see Gianmarco, but you don't think to call me to tell me what's happening...that you're safe...that Mariani didn't..."

"Then I went to Ryan's office." I figured I might as well get that out there too—I couldn't be in any deeper trouble.

"What?" Her question was sharp.

"I went to Ryan's office," I said.

"Again."

"Again, but I'm here now and I *am* sorry," I said. Ellen was angry, but there was a limit to how long she could stay angry and show that anger. Ellen was reaching that limit—I just had to push through to the other side. "There's this guy Vittorio de Santis at the office."

The waitress bought our coffee and something to eat. I wasn't sure what it was—I had let Ellen order; it seemed a small matter on which I could easily give way—but it involved pastry and it looked good. Not to mention, I had missed lunch. I took a bite. There was sweetness, there was almond, there was a flaky texture, and it all melted in my mouth.

"Good choice, sister," I said.

"You don't get out of the book of bad sisters by flattery," said Ellen flatly, then added, "This Vittorio character..."

"He said something strange. He said it must be obvious what's wrong in Ryan's life...so I should help him."

Ellen thought. "What's the nature of the relationship between Vittorio and Ryan?"

"I don't understand the question," I said. "Vittorio is a senior guy at the firm; Ryan does graphics. He designs packaging."

"And that's it?" asked Ellen. "Just two guys who occasionally meet in the office? Sometimes the boss says, 'Hey you, little person, design some packaging for me,' and that's it?"

"Well no, obviously Vittorio's got something to do with Ryan's disappearance—he wouldn't have said what he said if he didn't have a reason. But you're implying there's more."

Ellen frowned, gently shaking her head. "No. I'm asking what happened *before* what happened. What was the situation in which Ryan and Vittorio found themselves? If you're right that Vittorio is—to put it bluntly—at fault for Ryan's disappearance, then why did he choose to make Ryan disappear? Do you see what I'm trying to understand?"

I sighed. "Ever the historian."

"Ever the historian," she said. "But remember, historians are the only academics focused on fact."

I frowned.

"Scientists look at possibilities. Scientists look at the future. Historians look at facts—we want to know what actually happened. Two men in a room: What happened before—what baggage did they bring, and what did they then agree?"

The café was noisy, but Ellen and I fell quiet as she let me ponder her scenario.

"There's someone I want you to meet," I said.

Ellen was suspicious.

"There's a guy I met at the office. Tommaso. Vittorio was horrid to him. I need to apologize..."

"Why?" asked Ellen.

"Because he was humiliated in front of me and it's a kind thing to do. And because we need to talk with him."

"We?" Ellen seemed to be stuck on monosyllabic questions.

"We," I said. "You think differently from me."

There was a wry curl of her lip. "You mean I think, then act." She laid a hand on my hand and stared into my eyes. "You just react and react."

I might have been angry if I didn't know that what she was saying was correct. I retrieved my hand and grabbed my phone. "Tommaso Giordano," I said when the goddess answered.

nineteen

"There is a limit to how much coffee one person can drink in one day," said Ellen.

"That may be true," I said, "but by my reckoning that's only your third cup today, and a fourth won't hurt you. A fifth, however..."

Ellen was harrumphing. I ignored it. It was hard to differentiate between the harrumphing that was reasonable and the harrumphing because she was disgruntled with me, because I was focusing on Ryan's disappearance when I should be spending time with my sister who had left London and come to Genoa for the sole purpose of seeing me.

"I'm only here because this seems to be the only way I can spend time with you."

There it was. As we threaded our way through the narrow carrugi, heading for the café Tommaso had suggested—not too close to the office, but not too far away—Ellen had tried to guilt me again.

"Oh sis, come on," I said. "This is fun. This is dealing with real people. You're literally seeing history in the making."

There was some more harrumphing; then she asked, "Why are we meeting this Tommaso?"

"You'll like him," I said. "He's an angry, bitter, and twisted little man who can't even grow a proper beard. He thinks the world is against him...and it probably is."

"So why will I like him?" she asked.

"I don't think he's a bad person," I said. "I think he's quite a decent guy, really. But he's not a star, and everyone around him is better, faster, stronger, smarter.... He's one of life's also-rans, but he probably notices a lot because no one notices when he is there."

"An observer," said Ellen with a slight tone of wonder. "One who reports. He may be biased, but he feels it necessary to tell, rather than to keep secret."

"Precisely," I said as we reached the café. "And there he is."

Sitting at a table on his own was the scrawny man with a weak beard. Outside of his habitat of the office, he seemed twitchy, nervously scanning for predators.

He stood as he saw us enter. "Tommaso," I said, planting a small kiss on his cheek. He flinched. The show of affection didn't seem to upset him; he just wasn't accustomed to it, and he probably didn't trust it. "This is my sister, Ellen. She's helping me find Ryan."

He offered Ellen a limp hand as we sat.

"I wanted to apologize for you getting...bullied by Vittorio," I said.

He mumbled something. I think he said, "Not your fault."

"That's very kind of you, Tommaso. I..." The waitress interrupted. Apparently a decision around ordering coffee was a difficult challenge for Tommaso. For me, it was simple. For Ellen, it was even simpler: nothing.

When the waitress departed with our order, I continued. "I wanted to meet away from the office to make sure that Vittorio doesn't cause you any more hassle."

He said something—it was more that he was talking to himself than to me.

"I know you don't care about Ryan," I said. Tommaso seemed offended. "That sounded harsh. What I mean is, I know he's not necessarily your friend...not that you want to harm him."

Tommaso considered the notion, his head tilting from side to side as if there was a conversation going on inside that I wasn't privy to.

"Vittorio seems to be a different category of problem, and he seems to be a problem that impacts you." Tommaso nodded, agreeing with my assessment. "So let me help both of us. Tell me what you can about Vittorio." I was sure Ellen would tell me that this wasn't a subtle approach.

"Where to begin," said Tommaso, then shrunk back into himself. "No. I can't."

I leaned forward to encourage him but felt Ellen's hand on my shoulder. When she spoke, her voice was gentle, soothing. "You see things, don't you, Tommaso? You notice the details that no one else notices. What do you see? What do you hear?"

There was a pause; then Tommaso began, falteringly. "Debts. Debts that he can't pay to people you don't want to owe money to. And he's trying to earn the money to pay back what he owes by gambling."

"With Lorenzo Mariani?" I asked, feeling Ellen pinch me.

"No," said Tommaso. "I mean yes... He owes money... not to Mariani. Mariani's small—Vittorio owes money to big guys, you know...." He let the thought hang. "He didn't have stake money, so he did a deal with Mariani and traded Ryan's time. That's why Mariani doesn't show up as a client."

twenty

"Tell me about Gianmarco," said Ellen. "What did he say?"

She pulled the coffee Tommaso had left toward herself, as if to indicate to the waitress that she was a paying customer and not a hobo to be kicked out on the street.

"Ryan was typical Ryan," I said. "He threw himself into the relationship, completely and swiftly."

Ellen had that questioning look. It wasn't that she didn't believe—it was that she wanted some sort of quantification of terms like *completely* and *swiftly*.

"They met. Six weeks later Ryan had moved country and moved in with Gianmarco. And by the way, it wasn't that Ryan was a few miles over the border in France—he was living in the States. Logistically, that's not the simplest move."

As a historian, Ellen was used to hearing shocking details—that's maybe why she ended up focusing on the English constitution, although to hear her tell it, the history behind the development of the English constitution is as bloody as any history.

There's something she does when she's researching gruesome events that allows her to disconnect from what she's hearing. She dissociates from the suffering. Not because she's inhuman—quite the contrary: She's very humane, but to learn and understand the history, she has to move past a simple revulsion at the human horrors. She had heard what I said about Ryan, but to process it, she was dissociating on an emotional level.

"Gianmarco?" Ellen asked. "He was happy to move that fast."

"Yeah... I think he was.... But..." But what? "I don't know.... There's something not right in there. It's not one of them—it's both of them. I'm not convinced they've ever had a sensible conversation."

Ellen cocked her head. Tell me more, the movement said.

"I'm going to make an outrageous suggestion here," I said. "And I can't prove anything I'm going to say—it's just a feeling based on knowing Ryan since college and having spoken with Gianmarco..."

"Go on," said Ellen.

"I get the feeling that they both got into this thing really quickly—well, that's not a feeling, that's fact. But whenever anybody has raised a question or said 'what about' or 'slow down,' then Ryan and Gianmarco have got all huffy and ascribed the comment as anti-gay, rather than as someone trying to help. They've then been united in carrying on with their passion rather than talking to each other."

Ellen was nodding slowly. "Plausible. It sounds very plausible. But can I just reflect something back to you?"

"Reflect?"

"Just a thought." I shrugged, and Ellen continued. "You're suggesting that all is not well in paradise. Do you think that maybe—just maybe—this might be the cause, or at least a factor, in Ryan's disappearance?"

"No." I was surprised by the firmness of my response. "Did you not hear what Tommaso told us? Vittorio—he's the link."

"I heard," began Ellen. "But I..."

I stopped her. "I've met Vittorio—he's not pleasant; you'd understand if you'd met him. No, Tommaso was right; he's the link."

Ellen's lips were twitching, readying.

I knew she was just going to say something about caution, so I continued. "Can't you see how it fits together? Vittorio is Ryan's boss—or is a senior guy in the office who could make Ryan's life miserable—and he must have found out that Ryan is gay. Gay in a Catholic country—and I know Ryan wouldn't have come out to his colleagues until he felt safe discussing his sexuality. So this gives Vittorio leverage over Ryan, which is how he got Ryan to do this work for Lorenzo."

"That's a leap," said Ellen. "That's a huge leap."

"No it's not—it's obvious, isn't it?" I stood. "I need to talk to Vittorio properly. Will you come?" I could feel my breathing quicken and my heart kick up a beat or two.

Ellen lowered a hand. "Sit down, Monty." Her voice was calm, slow. "Pause for a moment. Think. Look at the other options here."

"What other options?" I asked, returning to my seat but rocking forward, lifting my bum off the seat while keeping a sitting position.

"Did you not hear what Tommaso said? This guy Vittorio—he may not be dangerous, but he seems to have dangerous friends."

"I just want to ask him some questions." It felt that I had to articulate each syllable. Ellen could be exasperating at times. She might be bright, but there were times when she just didn't catch on quickly enough.

She gave me her disappointed look. "This afternoon was for us to spend time together. I came here to see you. I can come here at any time—the history isn't going to go away."

She had played the guilt card and slipped it out from the bottom of the deck while I wasn't looking.

"Please," she said. "These people are dangerous. If you're so convinced that this guy is involved with Ryan's disappearance, then you should be going to the police."

twenty-one

Ellen had been upset—near tears upset—but had refused to come.

There were still a few hours of daylight, but the sun had long since started its path westward, leaving the narrow alley in shade. Where this morning, I had been able to sit cat-like and purr in the sun, now the early evening chill was finding its way through the city.

If the lack of sunlight had a benefit, it was that I could sit in the shadows, and without Ellen beside me, it was physically easier to push myself into a corner from where I could look out at the entrance to Ryan's office.

Tommaso was the first person leaving the office that I recognized. With his wispy beard, he looked stressed and earnest—too self-obsessed to notice anyone or anything around him.

Ten minutes later, Elisabetta bounced out of the door. She had a few words for the guy who held the door for her and shared a joke with the woman who followed her. She seemed to be noticing everyone and everything around her, saying warm goodnights to everyone as she lingered before departing. I pushed myself further into my corner, hoping I was invisible or at least sufficiently out of context that she wouldn't recognize me. After an age, she finally left, bouncing along the lane, stopping and chatting with everyone she passed.

The goddess, Carlotta Lombardi, was the next to leave. It wasn't just me—everybody thought she was a goddess. I was sure there were people throwing themselves on the ground so she wouldn't have to walk on rough cobbles. And as the aura surrounding the goddess passed, the alleyway became still.

I contemplated going in and searching out Vittorio, but

that seemed too fraught with opportunities for failure—doubtless everything was locked when the receptionist left—plus I wanted to know where Vittorio went. Maybe that would give me a hint about Ryan's location.

After an hour of waiting, there was still technically daylight overhead. If I remembered correctly, there were maybe two more hours of light. But in my shadowed corner, it was dark and the dampness of the alleyway was compounding the chill.

When Vittorio de Santis pushed his way through the door—a dark jacket covering his blue shirt—he looked tired. The muscles in his face seemed to have gone to bed half an hour earlier but had forgotten to switch off the lights and put the rest of the body to bed.

There was a moment of hesitation as he contemplated left or right—autopilot interrupted. He turned and started walking away from me. Slowly. A man walking because he needed to, not because he wanted to. A man walking without wanting to arrive.

His pace was inconvenient to follow, slower than my normal speed and just slow enough to be annoying. Usually I can drop my speed—take smaller steps, move my legs with less enthusiasm—but after an hour of standing in the cold, I wanted to move quickly to generate some warmth. The ascent helped, but not enough. Vittorio needed to move faster.

Vittorio also needed to go somewhere less unpleasant. As we ascended, the alleyways became narrower. I'm sure Ellen would've been able to notice architectural features that would differentiate each alley, but for me, I was following a man I didn't trust into a maze that was getting darker as the alleys narrowed, and I didn't have a loaf of bread to leave crumbs behind.

He took a right, another ascent. There was something familiar about the row of rundown shops—all of which had their metal shutters pulled down for the night.

And then Vittorio was gone. Shit.

I kept walking down the unfriendly alley, pausing to listen. All life appeared to have gone inside. Inside, where I should have been...with Ellen.

I spun to retrace my steps. Looking back down the street gave me a new perspective. The doorway on the left looked familiar, although when I had seen it, the door that was now closed had been open. Open and leading to a dark flight of stairs that came into Lorenzo's office. An office that didn't seem to be burdened with the tools of modern business: phones, computers, printers, and the like.

I scanned each side—there was nowhere to bury myself into the background, nowhere to nestle in the shadow and keep watch. I figured there was a fifty-fifty chance of Vittorio going in either direction, so I'd wait on the street, down from the doorway. If I was lucky, then he'd walk away from me. Unlucky, and I'd have to walk ahead and hope he didn't recognize me.

I waited less than five minutes. When the door opened two men came out. Vittorio was the first; the second I didn't recognize from my distance. He seemed shorter and wirier than I had expected Lorenzo Mariani to be, but then, I hadn't seen Mariani standing.

Vittorio's posture had changed. When he went into the building, he had been slouching. Now, he was standing straighter—it was as if he had puffed out his chest, figuratively and literally. Added to which he was now patting his jacket—that thing we all do when we put something valuable in a pocket and need to keep checking that it's still there. His right hand was lifting, double-tapping his left breast, lingering, and then dropping to repeat again after a few seconds.

The second man—possibly Lorenzo—finished locking the door and turned away from me; Vittorio followed, his hand rising every few seconds to check his pocket again.

I didn't think it possible for the alleyway to get narrower, but it did. I knew the buildings would all have been hues of orange, from near yellow to almost brown, but as I followed them—and we probably only walked about two- or three-hundred yards—with each step, the orange tone faded to gray as the overhead daylight strained its way into the narrow slit that the alleyway exposed to the sky.

The wiry man, who was probably Mariani, cast a furtive glance back before turning into doorway. De Santis followed without looking behind, and I became aware of being alone in a place I didn't know. There was an obvious route back— downhill until I reached the sea, then work my way to the harbor and find a landmark I recognized. But the thought of more narrow alleys—on my own, without Ellen, without anyone—seemed, to use Ellen's term, reckless, bordering on irresponsible.

That left me one option: wait.

As I reached the place where the two had disappeared, I found a rendered wall, probably orange, closed window shutters, and a door. A closed wooden door. Like its neighbors, the building was several floors high, maybe four or five, and unusually for an apartment block, showed no sign of habitation. Unlike most of the rest of the alleyway, this building was on a corner where two alleys crossed, and an intersection probably meant that I could find somewhere dark and out of obvious sight to wait.

twenty-two

The waiting didn't get more enjoyable. With each passing second I regretted that I hadn't listened to Ellen and wished that I had found some other way to approach Vittorio.

I did get to see other men arrive at the door. The procedure for entry seemed to be the same as de Santis and the man who was probably Mariani had followed: At the most, some made a furtive glance over their shoulder, but all disappeared in through the door, virtually without breaking step. There was no waiting, giving of passwords, or whatever—they entered.

After about an hour, a man left. The wiry man. As he came out of the door—which closed swiftly behind him—he paused on the threshold for a moment, readjusting to the temperature, the change in light, and the clean air of outside. The pause was long enough, and there was by then sufficient light reflecting along the alleyway that I could recognize Lorenzo Mariani before he turned and walked back toward his office.

After about two hours I became aware that I wasn't the only person in the alleyway. A few people had passed while I had been waiting. All seemed to move as if they had somewhere to go and wanted to be there as quickly as possible, but these two were ambling. Late teens, maybe early twenties, they were chatting as they walked, and from the sound of their conversation, they walked past the junction before realizing their mistake and returning.

On their return, they nervously fell quiet. Quiet being a relative term: They were quieter than they had been, but not as quiet as me and not as inconspicuous as me. As far as I could tell, while I had seen them and was aware of them, they hadn't seen me.

Some more people passed, more men entered the door,

one or two left—all looking dejected and downtrodden—and the breeze in the alleyways chilled the night further. It was probably somewhere around 11 PM when the door next opened. The procedure was becoming familiar: A man would step out, his shoulders hunched, his head slightly bowed and sometimes giving a small shake. To the extent that I could see facial expressions, the muscles around the mouth would always be pulled tight. The guy waited, acclimatizing to being outside, and then took in a large gulp of oxygen as he looked up—somehow in one move symbolizing defiance and defeat.

When he looked up, the face was familiar: Vittorio de Santis. But I wasn't the only one to have noticed—the two noisy guys who had been waiting for the last hour or so had clocked that it was someone they were meant to be paying attention to. They said nothing, but their movements were noisy: One slapped the other to get his attention; they both shuffled their feet to get a better position; and there was some sort of wordless conversation that involved hand gestures, head turns and points, and hunching of the shoulders.

I moved first.

They were busy going through some wannabe hard man ritual passed from age to age: That was my chance. A few quick paces, and I reached Vittorio. I slipped my arm into his: "A bit early to be leaving, isn't it?"

There was confusion in his face, but he didn't pull away. "You're...Ryan's friend."

"Montbretia," I said. "You seemed to have little difficulty recognizing me—and lecturing me back in the office."

"Montbretia, right," he said.

"Start walking," I said, pushing him to move. He held firm. "See those guys over there." I tossed my head in the direction of the noisy boys. "They've been waiting for the last hour, ninety minutes perhaps. The only time they've gotten interested is when you stepped out."

I pushed against him and he began to move, following back in the direction of Lorenzo's office. "Two of us changes the odds," I said, "and gives you a witness." He pulled me tighter—maybe it was agreement to the offer of company, maybe he was cold, or maybe he just liked women hanging on his arm. He picked up his pace, then turned into an alleyway on the left, letting the slope aid our speed.

The noisy boys were following. I didn't need to look around—I could hear their every step behind us. There was a shout—my Italian was nowhere near good enough and my grasp of noisy boy vernacular was nonexistent. I didn't know what they said, but it slowed de Santis, who wheeled around, came to a halt, and faced back toward the two. He didn't say anything, but he pulled me closer to him.

The noisy boys said something else. Again, I couldn't understand, but I recognized the bravado of male ignorance and stupidity.

"Not in front of my girl," said de Santis, as best I could translate. His voice was surprising confident given that I could feel how fast his heart was beating. "I'll be there tomorrow. Guaranteed."

The shorter of the two noisy boys approached. All cats are gray in the dark and all noisy boys are gray in the dark—all I could make out were the few reflections of lights catching his eyes and his teeth. "Tomorrow," he said, in what was clearly his best *big man menacing* voice. "Tomorrow...or *she* is in trouble." I didn't need a translator—his look and hand gestures told me everything.

The two turned and walked away from us.

As the alley regained its stillness, I became aware that de Santis was leaning on me, trembling.

twenty-three

When his heart rate had returned to something close to normal and his breathing had stabilized, Vittorio de Santis led us through more alleyways. Up to a point, I had thought I might be able to retrace my steps, but after this short walk, I was disoriented. Where I had previously felt secure that I could always walk down the hill to find the sea, somehow de Santis had managed to cross several junctions where we seemed to only have the option to ascend.

Maybe if I had GPS, maybe in daylight, things would be different. But for all intents and purposes, as I sat in the near empty bar that de Santis had led us to, I was lost.

"A beer," he said, placing two bottles on the table in front of me. He disappeared and returned a moment later. "Bread, olives. They don't do food here—the owner is doing me a favor."

"You know him?"

De Santis nodded.

"You trust him?"

Another nod.

"Do you owe him money, too?"

De Santis' seriousness relaxed and he sat across from me, picking up one of the bottles.

"I don't know where we are, so you're walking me back to my hotel. It's too late to be out on my own."

He bowed his head once to acknowledge.

The bar was small and dark. There were few lights, and the furniture all seemed to have been fashioned from dark wood. Maybe when it was filled with people talking or laughing it might have some character, but with just a few last stragglers leaning on the bar, it seemed to be the gloomiest place I had visited in Genoa.

"How many people do you owe money?" I asked.

He half smiled and took another swig of his beer. "Drink. Eat. It's good."

"How much do you owe?" His face fixed, so I continued. "People don't send street thugs to find and follow someone for fifty bucks."

He lowered his head, letting his chin come to rest on his hand, and balanced an elbow on the table to lever up his skull. The muscles in his face relaxed, and his eyes glistened.

"What do they think is going to happen tomorrow? What are they expecting from you?"

"Shhh," he said gently, closing his eyes and slowly shaking his head, his movement constrained as his chin was still resting on his hand, which in turn was propped up by his elbow on the table.

I picked at the olives—big, firm, green olives and smaller, more tender black olives, all with their pits still in place—and the bread, focaccia I thought, made with herbs and olives. The food didn't require concentration—it wasn't like a lump of meat where I needed to focus on cutting, or fish where there were bones to be avoided—so I kept my gaze locked on de Santis, occasionally reaching for an olive, or to tear some bread, or to sip my beer. This was the first food that I had seen for a few hours, and I wasn't going to ignore it. Also, I wondered whether de Santis was ready to talk.

But he sat, his eyes closed.

When his eyes opened, I was ready. "When we spoke in the office, you said I should help Ryan."

He didn't react.

"Ryan's missing. How can I help him? I want to *find* him, then I can help him."

"Find him...help him...words..." There was agitation in his tone. "You should...he's your friend."

"But you're his boss," I said. "You've been making him do work for Lorenzo Mariani that hasn't been billed. You've been using Ryan."

"I haven't." He seemed to crumple. Under the table his leg was twitching. "Why won't you help your friend?"

"You keep saying 'help,' but you don't say how I can help," I said.

"It's all the fault of his boyfriend." De Santis' face was reddening. "Doesn't he understand what Ryan has given up for him? Doesn't he see what Ryan has done for him?"

twenty-four

I had another beer and finished the bread and olives.

"They're local," said de Santis, but he only picked at them—he didn't have my hunger to keep eating. However, he did have a thirst: Where I had two beers, he had four. Maybe a fifth.

He slowly seemed to pull himself together. The scared child was progressively hidden behind his aggressive veneer, although his aggression seemed directed outward, not toward me. He talked a lot, but without specifics. A wide range of generalities with the subject changing frequently. There was talk about choices...options...half spoken in English and part in Italian. I struggled to keep up in either language, but it all seemed to come down to one fact: It wasn't his fault, apparently.

He didn't make another mention of Ryan, and I didn't ask.

He made good on our agreement and walked me back to my hotel. It took perhaps fifteen or twenty minutes and was a route I would never be able to find again, not that I would ever want to be alone in those dark alleys at 2 AM.

The alleys were largely deserted, although we did pass the occasional person. Usually a drunk, once a lost tourist who de Santis pointed toward a church the man said he could remember, a few whores—at least, I guessed they were—and the occasional unexplained fellow traveler down the narrow alleys. Once or twice I thought we were being followed, but there was never anyone behind us, so I put it down to my paranoia following our earlier brush with the noisy boys.

He walked me to the hotel entrance, shook my hand, and said goodnight. I watched him walk away, only going into the hotel when he had disappeared from my view.

The reception was dimly lit—it was the hotel equivalent

of a child's nightlight, there to offer some comfort if an unexpected guest appeared. On the far wall of the reception there was a small sofa. Square in design, the back and sides vertical and the seat perfectly horizontal. Square in design and not designed for comfort, as I found when I sat.

I wasn't ready for bed yet. Correct that: I was ready to get into bed, but I wasn't ready for sleep. It would be nice to be in bed and read for a while before turning out the light. But Ellen was in the room, and if I turned on the light and read, then I was likely to wake her, and if I woke her, then there was our not-quite-completed-but-now-worse disagreement to be continued.

So instead I sat in reception, waiting for sleep to come, and watched out the window at the few people walking and the odd cars passing.

"I'm sorry, I didn't see you there," said the night porter, shuffling in behind the desk, a coffee in one hand, a plate in the other, and a newspaper under his arm. "How can I help you?"

"I'm just..." I said absentmindedly. My gaze remained on the street, but something clicked in my brain. "On second thought, could you call me a cab?"

The night porter sucked air through his teeth.

"No urgency," I said.

There was the sound of rustling paper and tapping buttons, and then he spoke—fast Italian. He paused. "Ten minutes?" he asked.

"Perfect," I said.

The cab was there in eight, and the journey was equally speedy. "Wait here," I said, getting out without paying. It wasn't the height of good manners, but I wasn't going to walk home alone.

The stairs to the balcony were becoming familiar. I rapped on the door—loud enough to be heard inside, but not loud enough to cause a disturbance for the neighbors. In a few weeks when the temperature clicked a degree or two higher, people would sleep with their windows open. For the moment, they were closed to the disturbance I was causing.

A light. Sound. The door cracked. Gianmarco looked back at me. "Hi," I said. "Can I come in? I thought you might have some more dishes to be washed."

He smiled weakly and held the door open.

"I've got some questions about Ryan."

He led me through to a lounge, clicking on a low-powered side light as he passed. The light barely fell past the shade, but that seemed to be the only light that Gianmarco wanted as he continued into the room, dropping himself onto a large leather sofa.

The sofa had a younger sibling—a single-person chair, the only other seat in the room. I sat, feeling myself cuddled by the seat. It would be an exaggeration to say that the chair was the most comfortable chair I had ever sat in, but it was definitely in my top ten.

I had expected the two guys to have some borrowed bits of junk—maybe some hand-me-down sofas from Gianmarco's family—but these were new and expensive. You don't get furniture that feels this good from a bulk discount warehouse.

My night vision was becoming acclimatized to the dull glow from the light—not enough to be certain about the color of the sofa and seat, which I'm guessing were a shade of brown, but enough to see that the seating was disproportionately large for the room. Making another guess, I figured that was how the boys liked it. The room was small and dark—the seating accentuating both—giving a very womb-like experience.

"What has Ryan taken?" I asked.

This was clearly a perplexing question for Gianmarco, who shifted on the sofa, the skin on his legs occasionally squeaking on the leather. But this was the man who didn't wash his own dishes. I'm guessing that meant he didn't do the laundry or any other domestic chores, and that the details of anyone else's life would be a mystery to him.

"Ryan must have some luggage," I tried.

A grunt.

"Is any of that missing?"

There was a flick of Gianmarco's eye, caught by the yellow glow of the light. After a moment or two he said, "His Louis Vuitton overnight case isn't there."

"And did that disappear at the same time you last saw Ryan?"

He exhaled as if to say, "How the heck would I know?"

"You saw it when he was here. You don't recall seeing it since he's been gone. Is that a fair assessment?" I asked.

Another exhalation. This more like a teenager saying, "Yeah, I suppose, if I must, if you insist."

Then he spoke. A small, timid voice, afraid, embarrassed to be afraid: "Is he coming back?"

"Do you want him back?"

There was a small nod of his head, barely perceptible in the low light. His voice was almost a whisper now. "I love him."

"Love him...or love the rent?"

The sharpness of the reaction was unmistakable, even in the low light. His head spun and he stared at me. His voice was still quiet but had a new firmness. "I love Ryan."

twenty-five

I slept fitfully—it was the kind of sleep where you know you've been asleep, but you don't feel that you've been asleep and you don't feel refreshed for having been asleep.

The cab driver had been pretty grumpy about waiting. I threw him an extra €20 on top of the fare, and he shut up. It was probably around three when I got to the room, so I hadn't switched on the light. Now, with the first morning rays pushing their way around the curtains and into the room, I could make out the shape of the object I tripped over when I came in.

Ellen's case.

Ellen's case in a different place. Ellen's case not where I had put it when I unpacked it.

I slipped out of bed and opened the closet: Ellen's clothes were no longer there. The drawer where I had put the rest of her clothes, empty. I lifted the case; it was full, and was carrying her library.

My sister was going home. Soon. Today.

But not yet. The soft breathing as Ellen slept told me her flight wasn't for at least a few hours—if she had even booked her flight.

I padded across the room to her nightstand and knelt. I listened to her soft and rhythmic breathing—the way she only breathes when she's asleep—and reached for her phone, which was plugged in and charging.

I opened the alarm. It was set for 7 AM. Thirteen minutes.

Then I checked her email and text messages. I found the confirmations for the flight from London Gatwick to Genoa, but there was no confirmation of a return booking. That alone told me something about her anger—she wasn't even going to book in advance; she was going to go to the airport and would wait until there was a flight to take her home.

Shit. Worst sister ever. Worst sister, who was about to get even worse.

I reset the alarm on the phone for 10 AM.

Next I opened the nightstand drawer. Ellen was too predictable—but that was a good thing at the moment. I took out her wallet, removed the cash, and put it next to her phone. Then I grabbed her passport, too.

The dressing table, such as it was, had a small collection of tatty tourist brochures. Somewhere in there some hotel notepaper. I quickly scrawled a note:

ELLEN

YOU'RE ANGRY. I UNDERSTAND—IT'S MY FAULT. BUT YOU CAN'T LEAVE. LITERALLY, YOU CAN'T...

I'M GOING OUT TO GIVE YOU A CHANCE TO CALM DOWN WITHOUT ME UPSETTING YOU SOME MORE.

LOVE

MONTY XXX

A shit note, but there would be time for apologies.

I dragged on some clothes and picked up Ellen's wallet, which only contained her credit cards and her passport. At the reception desk, the night porter who had called me the cab was still on duty. "Signorina," he said.

"Could you put these in the safe, please?" I asked, handing him Ellen's wallet and passport.

"Certainly."

twenty-six

I might not have locked her up, but I was effectively holding Ellen hostage. She could leave the hotel room, she had cash, but she didn't have the means to get on a plane back to London.

If I had upset her enough that she was going leave, then taking her passport wasn't really going to be seen as ointment for the wound.

I worked my way down to the sea and slowly followed along the harbor edge. Genoa was waking up, but slowly. Everyone who was awake seemed to have a sense of mission—they were going somewhere, doing something now. Me? I was just wandering and wondering; looking out to sea as if my answer might come from a far-off land.

I passed a small café and took a coffee to go, then stood staring across the harbor, looking out to sea. The sun was up and offering some warmth, but it didn't seem to be trying very hard. It was like it was fulfilling some contractual obligation, rather than taking pleasure in its work.

The wind on the other hand, seemed to be an artist. It would blow gently; it would blow harder. It would push you this way; it would push you that. The one consistency with the wind was that it let you remember that you were not *quite* warm enough.

And that was good.

That slight bite kept me awake, made me think, made me focus.

Ellen had been right—I had been wrong. That went without saying by now. She told me to look at Ryan—I looked around Ryan. Until last night, I had been convinced that Vittorio de Santis had been the cause of Ryan's disappearance.

It seemed fairly obvious to me that de Santis had found

himself in financial trouble and had enlisted Ryan in his moneymaking scheme. Ryan would do some work for Lorenzo Mariani, Mariani would pay de Santis off the books, that money would become de Santis' stake money for the bigger game where he would try to earn back his losses. Ryan—the hapless employee—would be pressured by a senior guy and would have little option but to follow de Santis' instructions.

And I was still pretty sure that's how things started. But somewhere down the line Ryan had turned things. That was the irony—Ryan was being exploited because of his creativity, but it was another aspect of his creativity that he had found a way to twist the world to his advantage.

And Ryan had twisted the world by flipping the pressure back onto de Santis. He knew de Santis' weaknesses and had exploited them. How far and how much I wasn't sure—but I was sure that if Ryan had taken his Louis Vuitton overnight case, then he had intended to disappear.

And I had a pretty good idea that if I laid it out for de Santis, he would be able to tell me more. After all, he was a man who was susceptible to blackmail.

It was 8 AM when I reached the office. Eight AM, and hopefully Ellen was still sleeping. I still hadn't worked out what I was going to say to her.

The goddess was behind the reception desk, a deep red dress reverentially sculpting itself around every curve—worshiping, highlighting, exaggerating. A perfect package of bust, cleavage, waist, hips, and ass, wrapped in deep red.

Carlotta Lombardi sniffed. An un-goddess-like sniff. Crude, like a snot-nosed child without a care. Her tumbling curls pulsed along their length, showing their own vibrancy.

Another sniff, and Carlotta turned to me, a hand to her nose holding a clump of tissues. Her eyes were red, with tears flowing and makeup smeared.

"What's happened, Carlotta?" I asked reflexively, without considering the intrusion.

Another heavy sniff, a wipe of her nose, more tears.

When she spoke, her voice was hoarse, strained. "Vittorio," she said. "He's dead." She leaned forward, sobbing.

Something hit me in the gut and I found myself sitting, feeling winded. The guy I had spent several hours with last night—the guy who had walked my back to my hotel—was dead.

Every now and again, Carlotta reached out to somewhere under her desk, hidden from my view, and pulled another tissue, adding it to the clump in her hand. There were more sobs, sniffs, and the odd word or two, which was unintelligible.

After a few minutes, she threw the tissues into a trashcan, replacing the lump with three or four fresh ones before standing and patting down her face. Her breathing was fast, deep, and irregular, with her shoulders moving as she inhaled. Her cleavage quivered in sympathy.

When she looked to me, I wasn't sure what to say, so I said nothing. I hoped my face expressed sympathy and curiosity. Carlotta sniffed again.

I had to know. "What happened?" I asked.

"He was killed." She sniffed. "Last night...on the street... with a knife."

"That's awful," I said, feeling acutely how inadequate my words were. "Do they know...?"

Carlotta was shaking her head before I could finish my question, her mane swooshing from side to side. "No one knows why he was there, and no one knows why he was killed."

No one? I had an idea.

I also had a sister whom I needed to speak with.

twenty-seven

I was back before Ellen's alarm went off.

My strategy was simple: Get in, reset the alarm, and when Ellen complained about not waking when she intended, blame the phone. Shrug my shoulders and sympathize with her about the failures of technology. Perhaps ask her whether she put it on silent mode just to subtly shift the blame.

When I opened the door, Ellen was sitting on the side of her bed, holding the piece of hotel stationery on which I had scribbled my note. For the second time that morning, I was confronted by a tearful woman. With the first, I had no culpability—with the second, I was completely to blame.

"You stole my passport."

"I didn't steal it. I put it somewhere safe."

"Stole."

"And I took your credit cards and reset your alarm." If I was going to get shouted at, it was best to get everything out there.

She made a strange animal-like noise that broke into a sob before dashing into the bathroom, slamming the door behind her. I sat on my bed, waiting, listening to the sobs from the other side of the thin piece of wood.

There was the sound of a faucet running. It shut off, and a few moments later Ellen came out of the bathroom, her face damp but refreshed. The tears were gone, but her eyes were still pink.

"You won't spend time with me—in fact, it seems the most awful thing you could ever do in your life is to spend time with me—you won't listen to anything I say, but you won't let me go home and leave you to do whatever it is you obviously think I'm stopping you from doing. Explain to me how that's meant to make me happy." There was pain in her voice.

"We'll look back at this and laugh." I tried a jokey tone. Ellen's eyes moistened—the bravery she had found to come out of the bathroom and face me was crumbling. "I couldn't have you leave on such a sour note."

Something connected. Ellen was still angry—angry at me, disappointed in me, furious about what I had done today and since she had arrived—but something had connected. She had heard the truth I was trying to communicate. Nothing had changed, but she had heard me.

"I couldn't bear for you to go without us talking."

"And?" she said. Her eyes were moist, but there was a hint of mischief at the side of her mouth.

"And I need your help," I said.

She shook her head; her voice was a whisper. "You need to get past this obsession."

"You were right, Ellen. I found out so much last night." There was a look of concern spreading across her face. "Don't worry. I haven't been taking stupid risks—I made sure I was walked home last night."

"By whom?" she asked as if she felt obliged to ask but didn't actually *want* to ask, and definitely didn't want to hear the answer.

I went to my bed and sat, indicating Ellen should do likewise on hers. She declined. "Vittorio de Santis," I said. It wasn't the time for me to lie.

"The guy you think is responsible!" There was incomprehension in Ellen's voice. Anger. Frustration. She turned away from me.

"The guy who—if I'd listened to you..." I patted her bed to encourage her to sit. Slowly she began to move toward the bed. "If I had listened to you, then I would have figured out sooner that de Santis wasn't to blame."

Ellen sat on her bed, facing me, and raised her eyes as if to say, "Of course. It was obvious."

I continued. "De Santis had a gambling debt that was spiraling out of control and manipulated Ryan to help him. Ryan turned the tables and used de Santis' desperation against him."

Ellen remained still on her bed. She didn't need to say anything.

"But he's dead now," I said.

"Ryan?" Ellen was shocked.

"No. De Santis." I let the words hang, watching as Ellen took in the news that I had been trying to make sense of, realizing she was seeing the same issues I had seen, possibly being the last non-murderer to see him alive. "And yes, I am going to go to the cops—and I want you to come with me when I do—but first I need your help."

I don't know why, but the thought of talking to the police about de Santis scared me more than anything I could think of at that moment, and the realization of the poor man's death was starting to play on me. I wasn't at the level of Carlotta Lombardi's upset, but I could feel the tears starting to form.

I didn't hear her move, but I felt Ellen's arms wrap around me.

twenty-eight

"I'm paying," I said as we watched the waitress disappear with our order.

"It's alright," said Ellen. "The thief who took my wallet and passport was kind enough to leave my cash behind. Where are they, by the way?"

"Oh." I felt the shock, realizing I hadn't retrieved Ellen's possessions. Involuntarily, I felt my hand cover my mouth. "I'm paying because... Because I am. And your stuff is in the hotel safe."

"I didn't realize we were in such an upmarket hotel that it actually has a safe."

I shrugged. "I didn't check it myself—I'm guessing it's just a drawer somewhere in an office. It's probably got a big Keep Out sticker on the front for added security."

The café was more for tourists than for locals, and around us there was the constant clatter of foreigners in a foreign land, who seemed to find the notion of sitting on a chair at a table to be a new and different experience. Apparently this was the sort of thing that no one had warned them about when they booked their trip on the internet.

I broke the quiet between Ellen and me. "I was convinced it was de Santis."

"I know," she said softly.

"But I saw when I looked into his eyes: There was desperation. He wanted me to help Ryan, not for Ryan, but for himself."

Ellen was listening but didn't seem to be of a mood to remind me about my stupidity.

"Those two thugs had already worried him enough," I continued.

"Thugs?" asked Ellen, her voice not quite as calm.

"Slow down," I said. "Not thugs. I exaggerate." Now was

not the time to tell Ellen the full details of last night. "He was threatened last night. Nothing serious."

"He's dead." Ellen cut me off. "It was serious."

"But he didn't think so at the time—he thought it was just two kids who he shooed away. He wasn't worried about them. There was more...and Ryan figured in it."

Ellen had returned to her listening mode.

"I still don't get it," I said. "Ryan has bolted with his treasured Louis Vuitton suitcase in hand."

"Wait," said Ellen.

"Yes," I said, before she could ask the question I knew she was going to ask. "Ryan disappeared himself. But I reckon someone must have been helping him since then. I thought it was de Santis, but it was clear last night that there's someone else, and I don't know who that is."

"Easy," said Ellen. "Who's the person with everything to gain and little to lose? Who benefits from Ryan being out of the picture?"

"No," I said, then caught myself. Ellen had been right so far. "Really?" It sounded like a question, but in truth I was making noise as I processed what Ellen had said. If—for once—I assumed she was right and worked from there, then who would benefit from Ryan disappearing?

Ellen waited, watching me. I guess she thought I was going to say something, so she jumped in first. "The challenge isn't to figure out who has been helping Ryan."

"It isn't?"

She laughed at the simplicity of my retort. "No. You just have to watch the body language when they're challenged. They might protest their innocence in the matter—but their reaction will always give them away."

"Oh," I said, continuing hesitantly. "So what is the challenge?"

"To persuade them to lead you to Ryan." She sat back in her seat. She had that look she gets when she's trying not to sound too triumphant.

A family with four kids pushed their way through the

door. The father looked aggressive, the mother haggard, the two taller kids—perhaps twins—resentful, the third bemused, and the fourth, a boy of about five, really excited. Seemingly this was an opportunity for ice cream. Ice cream and noise. The decibel level rose as the parents shared their mistake with the room.

I looked back to Ellen. "How do you do that? How do I persuade whoever it is—that you apparently know has helped Ryan, but I'm still guessing at—to give up Ryan?"

"History teaches us," said Ellen, smirking, "that it's all about what they've got to lose. More specifically, what they *think* they've got to lose. If there's more to lose by protecting Ryan than by giving him up, then they'll give him up."

Ellen was being infuriating. She had a point—a good point, laid out in terms she knew I couldn't argue with—but she wasn't letting on who had helped Ryan. She didn't even hint by letting the gender slip.

"You know who it is?" I asked.

"Oh yeah," she said.

"Then you're going to have to come with me, sis. You need to do the talking—you've got this stuff figured out, and I'll just get angry.

"First," she said, "breakfast."

I nodded.

"And once we've finished breakfast, I'll tell you who it is."

twenty-nine

We stood in the sun—two purring cats enjoying the warmth—and waited.

"You don't think we should go in?" asked Ellen.

"Too many unhappy people. Anyway, I've called—he'll come out." A slight note of anxiety hit me. "You are sure that it's him?"

"Little to lose, a lot to gain…a sniveling coward… Yeah, it's him." I loved when Ellen was this confident and logical.

"But how are you so certain?" I asked.

"Look at what he got," said Ellen. "By befriending Ryan he got the direct connection to Vittorio which gave him the inside gossip. He got the inside line on Vittorio, the man who was tormenting him. And when Ryan compromised his own employment by going AWOL, he lined himself up to be top dog again, or number-two mutt after that Elisabetta woman."

"Makes sense," I said. "And you're happy to do the talking?"

A single bob of her head affirmed.

The office door opened and he stepped out, pushing the cuffs of his black turtleneck away from his wrists. With his weak beard, he clearly thought he had captured the vibe of a Silicon Valley entrepreneur.

"Thanks for meeting us," I said. "Sad day."

Tommaso's face contorted. He had seemed pleased—almost excited—to come out and meet me, but when I reminded him about Vittorio de Santis' death, the enthusiasm was replaced by a socially acceptable mask of shock and grief.

"You're not going to tell us that you're sad," said Ellen.

Tommaso's face contorted again. He hadn't expected Ellen to speak, and clearly he was surprised by her bluntness.

There was a flash of anger across his face, almost as if he wanted to say, "How dare you?" This gave way to the realization that he had just betrayed a dark feeling held deeply inside, festering. Finally, his face reddened. A naughty boy, caught.

"I'll get to the point," said Ellen, without giving Tommaso the opportunity to explain his reaction. "We've just come from the police; they think it was you."

The embarrassment was gone in an instant, to be replaced by shock. Shock giving way to anger and fear. "What?" asked Tommaso.

"Monty saw Vittorio de Santis yesterday. You were there. You saw that they had words. She saw him again later, outside the office."

Tommaso didn't seem to understand what Ellen was trying to convey.

"Don't you understand?" said Ellen. Tommaso shook his head slowly. "Monty argued with a man who ended up dead. That makes her a suspect."

There was a creeping realization crossing Tommaso's face. We weren't there to talk about him—this wasn't about him.

"But Monty didn't do it."

"Of course," said Tommaso with no sincerity.

"So we need to clear her," continued Ellen. "And the way to clear her is to point the cops to the person who committed the crime."

Tommaso seemed torn. On one hand he looked as if he wanted to agree with Ellen and her straightforward logic. On the other, he was being cautious, which was quite reasonable given that Ellen had told him that the police wondered whether I was involved with the murder.

"We know what happens when Americans get suspected of murder in Italy," said Ellen. "I don't want to spend the next five years proving Monty is innocent while she sits in a jail. So unless you've got an alibi for last night, then we've got to tell the cops that you hated de Santis and murdered him."

"It wasn't me," gushed Tommaso, his voice fast and

trembling. "You can't say it was me just because you don't want your sister to go to jail. No...it's not...I'm not..." He turned as if to leave.

"Stop," said Ellen. "We're trying to help you."

Tommaso looked confused.

"If we can say to the police it wasn't you, then that's good, isn't it?"

Tommaso still looked confused, but more because he didn't understand Ellen's point.

"Think about it. If the cops arrest you and you say, 'I didn't do it,' then they're going to think you're like every other guilty man who denies everything. But if Monty says it wasn't you, the cops are far more likely to believe that. The suspect who could throw everything on you, but who instead says that you're innocent...that's far more compelling."

Tommaso's mouth formed into an "O" shape. The sides of the O twitched as an escape hatch seemed to come within reach.

"We just need to make sure you've got a solid alibi for last night," said Ellen.

thirty

"I'm getting bored of cafés," I said. "And this is a boring café."

Ellen stared but said nothing. There was nothing she could say. It was a tedious café—everything seemed to have once been white but now wasn't. Any character there might have once been—however slight—had now left.

I looked across the dulled melamine surface of the table—once gleaming, but now pitted and yellowed—and asked, "Is he going to bring him?"

Ellen bobbed her head once. Absolute certainty.

"He hasn't just left us here and done a runner?"

"He'll bring Ryan," she said, calmly and without emotion. "Any delay will be brought about by Ryan."

Which was Ellen's way of saying she suspected Ryan's behavior would be theatrical...histrionic. I wanted to tell her she was wrong.

But she was right.

"Tommaso hasn't got that much to lose by giving up Ryan."

"Office gossip? Top-dog status?" I butted in.

"Without Ryan in the office, there's no source of gossip for Tommaso, and if he thinks the disappearance is enough to get Ryan fired, then Tommaso is already top dog again." Ellen watched, waiting until I had processed, then continued. "But he thinks he's got a lot to lose by not giving him up. Ryan, however, has much to lose from coming here. Ultimately, he's got to lose face, although he will try to minimize that."

"You mean by lying."

"Lying, minimizing, framing himself as the victim, refusing to take responsibility. You name it," she said.

We fell into an uneasy quiet, which was broken when the

door swung open. Tommaso stood, holding the door and looking behind him. He waited nearly thirty seconds until reluctantly, Ryan stepped into the café.

I had always held a vision in my mind of Ryan being a bit chubby. He was never overweight, but when I first met him, he still had a layer of puppy fat. That excess had been worked off before I left college, leaving a healthy young man, but the image of the chubby kid stayed.

Ryan looked down, not making eye contact with anyone. His hair—slightly long, slightly foppish—fell over his eyes as he turned and lowered his head. He seemed in no hurry to remove this shield.

Ellen stood. I went to follow and felt her hand gently keeping me in place. She might have said something to the two men—I wasn't sure—but then she was helping Ryan into her seat across the table from me, as if she were helping a grandmother.

Ryan sat impassively, not making eye contact and not speaking. I looked up and caught the door swinging closed behind Ellen, who had led Tommaso out of the café. I felt a sudden dread, a nervousness, a tingling of my skin followed by the clamminess of sweat, the beating of my heart, and the unsteadiness of my breathing.

Ellen was meant to be here. Ellen was meant to do the talking. But Ellen was letting me know that this was my problem—it was time for me to fix it.

Finally Ryan looked up. He had the sneer of a surly, defiant teenager who had scraped the car on the gatepost and was arguing that it was the gatepost's fault.

"You couldn't make him love you, so you made him miss you." I found the anger in my voice shocking. I was expecting that I would have trouble controlling my emotions—that was part of the reason why I wanted Ellen to talk—but still I was shocked by how raw and close to the surface my emotions were.

"You flounced out of the apartment you share with Gianmarco." My voice was becoming more controlled, but somehow my anger was welling. "All you've tried to do is to control other people."

Ryan shook his head. When he stilled, a deep frown remained.

"Here's how I see it. Tell me if I get anything wrong," I said. "Gianmarco broke up with you. You felt bad. You felt rejected. And you wanted to make Gianmarco regret the breakup. You wanted him to feel bad—you wanted him to feel what you were feeling. You knew that if you went missing, then Gianmarco would have to notice, eventually... And by the way, Gianmarco is beautiful."

Ryan's frown fell away, and his face softened. Not quite a smile—more than that, more like complete serenity crossed his face as he stared as if looking a thousand miles out to sea.

"But you didn't want Gianmarco just to notice that the dishes hadn't been cleaned or his laundry hadn't be done, you wanted him to be worried. You wanted him to miss you. You wanted him to want you back. You wanted him to think that your disappearance was his fault. And then I stumbled into Genoa, and you saw an opportunity."

Ryan gave a wiggle of his head worthy of any actress trying to resettle her hair, and then ran a finger to push the last few strands behind his ear. He still wouldn't make eye contact.

"You figured that I would be worried and would immediately start asking questions and banging on doors. It would only be a matter of time before I turned up at your apartment looking for you, and then bingo! Gianmarco would see that you had really gone and would get worried. Your reckoning was that I would be there and I would tell Gianmarco that it was his fault."

A slight flush of crimson was pushing its way onto Ryan's cheeks. Under the table his leg was twitching, reminding me of Vittorio de Santis last night.

"You thought I'd fix everything for you."

"Did he miss me?" asked Ryan.

I let the question hang, finally able to make eye contact

with my friend who, at that point, I would happily have slapped. "See—selfish," I said. "Next you'll be asking me whether he's agreed to get married or whether he's thought any more about adoption."

The slight flushing of his cheeks turned into a full crimson, and we lost eye contact as he dropped his head.

"These are not questions you should be asking me, Ryan. These are discussions you need to have with Gianmarco." I kicked him gently under the table. "You need to talk with Gianmarco. You need to be a big boy."

He looked up. There was a moistening in his eyes, but he said nothing.

"If the effort you devoted to trying to make other people sort your life out for you was refocused on working on yourself and your relationship with Gianmarco, then the two of you might stand a chance. But if you don't work on the relationship—together—then there is no relationship."

He started blubbering.

thirty-one

Ryan pulled the Louis Vuitton overnight case as if he was being paid to model it. Of the few people who passed us, no one seemed to care or even notice.

I would describe the case as purple, but apparently that was wrong and was an insult to the label, which I should join in worshipping. It wasn't purple, it was gentian, anil, deep indigo, or dirty azure, or something. Honestly, I didn't care and I wasn't in a mood for having that conversation. To me, luggage had a function, and as long as it performed that function, then I was happy.

Reverentially, Ryan carried the case up the stairs and then returned it to the ground to take the few steps to the door of the apartment he had once shared—and might still share—with Gianmarco.

He had been nervous about returning. I had called him out on his bad behavior, and his only defense had been tears and to plead forgiveness. In short, he did anything he could to deflect away from his behavior.

"I can't," said Ryan, stopping halfway along the passage. "I can't. He's never going to forgive me." Then he started mumbling. Well, he may have been talking. I just stopped listening; I have a limit for how much self-indulgence I can tolerate. My limit with Ryan had long been passed, even before Tommaso dragged him to the café.

It was around 1 PM. Gianmarco should be awake. However, it was unlikely that he would be dressed in more than a toweling robe.

I rapped on the door and waited. It seemed rather odd to me—Ryan should have a key, but by approaching this way we could establish who had territorial rights. I rapped again and heard the sound of feet coming toward the door.

Ryan was clutching the handle of his case, his hand

trembling, his head bowed.

The door opened. Gianmarco looked at me and half smiled, seemingly unable to find words to acknowledge my presence and not wanting to spend the mental energy required to think why I might be there. Ryan looked ready to run. I reached, grabbed his coat, and pulled him into Gianmarco's view.

There was a gasp, the door was knocked open, and then a range of moist sounds. There was a singular lump of two men embracing. I turned away to give them some privacy and looked down over the street, its shades of orange bathed in bright sunlight.

After maybe two or three minutes, I turned. The two were still embracing with their mouths locked. I lifted the case, took it inside the apartment, and closed the door behind me. I wondered whether Ryan expected me to bow to the case as one would be expected to bow to a member of a royal family or a head of state, but I decided against.

My entrance had not disturbed the two.

I clapped my hands loudly. Three quick claps. "Boys, boys, boys!"

No reaction.

I grabbed each by the hair and pulled, physically dragging their mouths apart. Ryan went to complain but stopped when he caught my eye. I kept my gaze fixed on him, and he released Gianmarco, taking a step away from the other man.

I released their hair and found myself in a triangle, each of us uneasily looking at the other. Gianmarco had literally rolled out of bed and was now covered in Ryan's slobber, but he was looking more beautiful than he had ever before. He was almost physically glowing, he was so beautiful.

I pointed a finger at each of them. "Boys," I said sternly. "It's good that everyone's back home, but we've got some work to do. Ryan was a stupid child..." Gianmarco puffed up his chest. "Don't you start," I said to him. "You're a nightmare to live with. I've never lived here, but I've worked that one out already." I spun back to Ryan. "You're a nightmare, too. You're my friend—but you're a nightmare."

The two stood silently, two scolded children who were trying not to laugh while teacher was getting stern.

"You need to talk. The two of you. One says something, the other listens and then replies. Stop reacting; start listening. And if anything goes wrong, blame yourself, not the world. And if you can't sort things out, then find a counselor."

That was enough. They had stopped listening, so I left. If I hadn't closed the door behind me, they wouldn't have noticed.

thirty-two

"I thought you were going to bring me somewhere impressive," I said, unable to draw my eyes away from the ceiling.

Ellen pretended she was readying herself to punch me.

"Hey! Not in church."

"It's not a church." Ellen spoke with her teeth held firmly together, but unable to keep the grin off her face. She knew I was goofing off. "It's a cathedral. Basilica della Santissima Annunziata del Vastato."

"And that gets you a better quality of god, right? Your prayers actually get answered here?"

"Shut up and follow me," she said, leading me to the central aisle with pews on either side. Simple wooden seats, probably less than five years old, in a basilica where construction began in the sixteenth century. "Sit." Ellen indicated an empty row. I sat. "Look up."

The façade of the basilica was comparatively simple. Sure, it was big and imposing with columns, towers, and the like, but at the end of the day, it was some light-colored stone cut into straight lines. I liked it. I liked the simplicity. But it wasn't something that had the wow factor that those annoying women on the home-design programs always talk about.

Inside, however—looking up at the vaulted ceiling—the only word was wow. I would have liked to be able to say more, but I lacked the vocabulary. It was so far beyond my experiences that I couldn't find words to describe what I was feeling as I stared up.

The pillars supporting the roof were simple in their design with some ornamentation at the top. The plain stone was in stark contrast to what it supported. The dominant feature of the ceiling was gold. In a city of orange, here was gold—unambiguous gold. Gold nearly everywhere, and framing artwork painted onto the barreled ceiling. Each piece of artwork depicting a religious scene, most with Jesus and angels.

"So are the boys settled?" Ellen broke my concentration.

"Who knows," I said without letting my eyes leave the ceiling. "I got them together in the same apartment—that's my job done. I'm sure they'll be fine for the next day or so, and I'm sure they'll use a lot of lubricant...heck, I'm sure a lot of lubricant has already been used."

Ellen pinched me.

"What? If He was that upset, then this is the place I'd get struck down." I let my eyes continue to follow the ceiling, taking in each individual tiny detail that the artists and craftsmen had labored over several hundred years ago. "Elisabetta called while I was on my way over. Wanted to tell me about Vittorio," I said. "Apparently the police think it was wrong place, wrong time—maybe a mugging gone wrong. They don't seem to have made a link with his gambling."

"Oh," said Ellen softly.

"What about Tommaso?" I asked. "How was he?"

"He was fine," said Ellen. "He was a lot less anxious, and I made sure he didn't feel too bad what with me telling him we'd talked to the police and were ready to lead them to him."

"My sister the liar," I whispered and turned to face her. "So where are you taking me tomorrow? Genoa's a historic city, if you didn't know—famous for giving the world Christopher Columbus, jeans, and pesto, not to mention a huge trove of art and all this architecture. If only I knew someone with a book..."

Ellen pinched me again.

"You're going to stay?" It was a statement, but I let it sound like question.

"I've got a meeting next Thursday that I have to be back for, so I'm here until Wednesday." She paused. "Unless you upset me before then."

"I'm sorry," I whispered.

"All's forgiven," she said. "But you will come to London in May. Nigel will be busy launching his book, so he'll be completely intolerable going on about this PR guy Boni-whatever-his-name-is. I'll need some sanity in my life."

Note from the Author

I hope you enjoyed this book. If you want to know more about me and my books, then join my readers' group.

When you join, I'll send you my introductory library and add you to my readers' group mailing list. Every month I'll send you my communiqué, Simon Says. This includes news about my books, special offers, and extracts, together with a few pieces I think you may find interesting.

Join my readers' group and get your free books here: simoncann.com/readers.

About the Author

Simon Cann is the author of the Boniface, Montbretia Armstrong, and Leathan Wilkey books.

In addition to his fiction, Simon has written a range of music-related and business-related books, including the How to Make a Noise series, the most widely ready series about synthesizer sound programming, and Made it in China, about entrepreneurs building businesses in China. He has also worked as a ghostwriter on a number of books.

Before turning full-time to writing, Simon worked as a management consultant, where his clients included aeronautical, pharmaceutical, defense, financial services, chemical, entertainment, and broadcasting companies.

He lives in London.

You can find more about Simon at his website: simoncann.com.

www.ingramcontent.com/pod-product-compliance
Lightning Source LLC
Chambersburg PA
CBHW020310150626
46552CB00022B/2583